S0-AJN-395

jasmine in my hand

A NOVEL BY

MUS WHITE

SUN  WEPT PRESS

Copyright © 2006 Mus White

All rights reserved. This book, or parts thereof, may not be reproduced in any form without permission.

Sunswept Press
P.O. Box 1664
Los Angeles, California 91614

www.sunsweptpress.com

Library of Congress Cataloging-in-Publication Data

White, Mus

Jasmine in My Hand/Mus White

ISBN 0-9768804-0-7

First Edition

Foreign Rights:
Intellectual Property Group
9200 Sunset Boulevard, Suite 520
Los Angeles, California 90069

Printed in the United States of America
by The Castle Press, Pasadena, California

Book and Cover Design by Betty Adair

In Memory of My Parents

HELGA ELEANORA VICTORIA SKOV
1909-1972

EGO EILER SKOV
1909-1979

CHAPTER 1

Sim sela dim bam ba sela du sela dim. The call of the crow casts its voodoo spell, and then...Pia is gone. One letter swapped, and "Pia" is now "Pea." Jeffrey, my husband of thirty-seven years and the father of my two daughters, names me Pea when we first meet. Waving his magic wand, Jeffrey transforms my fanciful Princess Pia, asleep in her fairy tale, to the pea hidden under the mattress. He thinks it's funny that he can alter the meaning of my name, as well as my stature, with the change of one little vowel. Oh, so funny it is.

Tired of the joke, I have lost my sense of humor when it comes to my husband's artfulness. Jeffrey, on the other hand, doesn't appear altogether displeased with his role as magician. Yet, if you listen carefully, the tone of his voice sounds faintly pinched when he thanks me for making him into a prince at the end of my tale. My own sorcerous craft doesn't make him come to life as often as he wishes. He is unhappy with the dance.

"Hey, I'm here, too," he laments, with a small pout in his voice.

"Don't worry. You are my treasure," I tell him.

I don't tell him that I want to pick him up by the ear and drop him into my jewelry box. I don't say, "I want to keep you all to myself next to my diamond tiara."

I look in the mirror and ask myself: "Does it matter? Does it matter what I say? Do I, in any way, matter on this earth of ours that hangs in empty space below the northern sky stretching as far as God's hand can reach?" I smile at my conceit. Oh, such pompous thoughts.

Why? Why me? Why do I have to speak? It's outrageous that the monster won't stop pulling me out of bed. How dare it pull me by my hair? First chance, I'll hurl my ax at its head. I promise. Can't the moron see that I have a piece of amber stuck in my mouth that keeps me from speaking? Stop. Stop pulling, and I will tell. I'll tell all. I promise.

The face in the mirror above the white porcelain sink reveals the face of a granny. Faint lines fan out from the eyes, reaching for the blond hair that grows gray at the temples. I see the little crevice at the corner of the mouth. I see the chin drooping just a little. I see the two red rings that circle the neck and the once apple-green eyes now faded.

"Get a grip, you old hag," I scold the reflection in the mirror. "Get a grip, you ungrateful witch. What's the matter with you? You have it all. Shame on you. Go back to your king-size bed. Pray for mercy. Pray for forgiveness. Go back to your bed, you old granny."

I go back to my king-size bed and close my eyes. I think back to the hour of lost faith. I think back to the hour when we grasp that the world is not flat and straight. I think about the skein of yarn held loosely between two hands. I think about the hours shaping the ball of yarn that we unravel.

I think about the sweet cool air of the evening. I think about the wind that blows clear blue across the glaciers. I think about loss and death. I think about the laughter and the ghosts across the table. I think about the time, fifty years ago, when I was a child of seven in Denmark.

I see the child running with the wind in her face. She runs with the speed of the deer fleeing the fire behind her. The trees fly past her in a green blur. Wet with terror, she feels her hair sticking to her head. She hears her heart pounding. She is the mouse who senses the claw of the eagle upon its back. She hears the tom-tom drum of feet behind her. She doesn't look back. She is running for her life.

She flees to a high pile of cut trees. Gathered in the back of the woods, the pile looks to her as tall as the building at home on the street. She climbs on top of the trees and falls down into a hole. You can hear her prayer.

Please, listen.

CHAPTER 2

"Oh, my God. Give me my mommy," the child prays aloud, stumbling down the other side of the pile of branches. She rolls down again, now hitting the ground with a thump. She clasps her hands toward her Father in heaven. She prays on her knees that God will hear her. He must answer her prayers. He will protect her.

"Please, dear Father in heaven. Don't let them find me. Please, give me back my mommy."

"Pray, pray and you shall get. Pray," says the pastor in Sunday school. "Never pray for a bicycle. Don't pray for money to buy candy. Never pray for steak and potatoes with gravy. Don't ever pray for an orange. Don't pray for a new hat.

"Pray for food for the starving children in China. Pray for peace in the world. Pray for the sick children in Africa. Pray for mercy. Pray for forgiveness."

She prays for mercy. She prays for her mommy. She promises God, "I'll be good."

She hears the steps of a thousand cowboys pounding closer. She looks down upon the pine needles spread in a thick blanket over the ground. Her prayer is over. She hears them yodel with hands that flap fast over their mouths. She hears the sounds of Indian war cries. The cowboys holler, "Yoo hoo hoo." She is here with cowboys who don't even know how to be cowboys.

The cowboys see her hiding behind the pile of cut trees. They pull her up, dragging her bare legs through the dry pine needles. Her brown skirt pulls up over her white cotton underpants. The cowboys pull her by her arms and her hair. They tie her to a tree and are about to cut her hair off and slash her face with a knife when they hear the sound of the whistle. The teacher blows her whistle again: lunchtime.

The cowboys run off. They leave the Indian tied to the tree to be eaten alive by bugs and ants. Bugs and ants will eat her alive. The child prays for mercy. She prays for forgiveness. Her God has left her behind. No God would have left her tied to a tree. She is seven, and she knows there is no God. There is no God in heaven.

The cowboys have left the Indian behind to die alone without her mommy. But rather than entering a heaven with no God, she wiggles herself loose from the tree. She brushes off the pine needles stuck to her brown skirt. She picks the needles out of her gray kneesocks that have fallen down to her ankles. Her white skin is scratched and bruised.

She crosses the gravel raked in front of the white building with the high black roof. She walks up the front stairs and opens the big black door. She walks to the right into the dining room where she sees forty kids sitting in silence at the long tables. She sees them stuffing themselves with liver and onions and potatoes covered in thick brown gravy. She knows they don't care if she is eaten alive by bugs and ants under the tree. They don't care.

Mrs. Andersen's gray eyes glare at her below lids that fall wrinkled like dried leaves. "You are late," Mrs. Andersen aims her voice at her. "Go to the little table over there in the corner. Eat by yourself, you naughty girl."

The child slinks over to the little table in the corner while she makes an effort to pull up her gray kneesocks. She sits down with her head bent low over her plate and silently eats her fried liver with onions and her boiled potatoes smothered in thick brown gravy. She loves liver with onions.

She loves the taste of thick brown gravy on boiled white potatoes. The kids eat their vanilla pudding with caramel sauce while she silently eats the liver. She is not sad. She likes to eat by herself in peace. "No dessert for you today, you naughty girl."

"You naughty girl," Mrs. Andersen repeats. The child takes a sip of her thick sweet buttermilk and remembers herself at home sitting on the kitchen counter and drinking a glass of buttermilk. She begs her mother to let her go away from home. "Please, Mommy, let me go. Please, let me go," she begs.

She hears her mother talk with Mr. Jensen at Princess Street School. He tells her mother he doesn't think it's a good idea for Pia to go away. She hears him say, "That place is for kids from the street. That place is for kids with no beds and no food. That place is for kids with drunken parents. That place is for kids who need the sun and fat on their ribs. It's not the right place for Pia."

"I need it," the child insists. Her mother is not sure. The child knows that her mother loves her the best in this world. She knows that in the end she always gets what she wants from her mother. Her mother will even let her go away if she wishes to go. Her mother will let her part from her if that is what she wants to do.

"I am sure I want to go. I want it," the child pleads with her mother. She wants the sun. She wants the fat on her ribs. She wants the country air. She wants to get away from the street. She pleads with her mother, "Please, let me go."

"I need it, Mommy. See my eczema. See how bad it is. I need

the sun. If I'm in the sun in the country, I won't have to take the streetcar to Finsen's Institute in the morning anymore. I won't need to lie naked with my green goggles under the lights. I won't have to lie next to the naked fat lady with the brown warts on her breasts that hang like two giant bells down to her navel. I won't have to smell the tar soap and smear the black tar cream on my legs any longer. Please, Mommy, let me go," she begs her mother.

Her mother lets her go. Now, Pia feels as if she is a prisoner in Klint on the island of Zealand for the rest of her life. She is here eating liver and onions at a small table by herself. She is here with kids who don't know how to cradle a spoon gently between the thumb and the forefinger. She is with kids who hold the fork like a stake in the hand.

She is here with kids who don't wipe their bottoms and who wet their beds at night. She is with kids who fight; kids who don't know God; kids who don't listen to the teachers; kids who throw stones; kids who pick green snot out of their noses; kids who don't know how to line up and curtsy nicely. She is here with kids from the street.

"Please, Mommy. Please, pick me up. I made a mistake. Mr. Jensen was right. I don't belong here. Please, let me come home. I don't need the sun. I don't need to get fat. Bring me home. I don't need the country air. I'm afraid of the kids. They tear out my hair. Here's a chunk of my hair," she writes to her mother and father in one of her letters.

"Here's a chunk of my hair," she writes, folding a chunk of her hair in a piece of toilet paper for them to see. "I put it in the envelope for you to see. You can see for yourself that they tore out my hair. They broke my front tooth with a stone. Please,

Mommy. Let me come home. I'll never ask you for anything again. I will be good."

Her mother never comes. Forgetting the doubts she had when she first spoke to Mr. Jensen, her mother says to herself at home, "Oh, the country. It's so good for Pia to be in the country. The air will make her grow big and strong. The air will bring back the red in her cheeks."

The child sits on the white stucco fence that faces the road while she waits for the country air to turn her cheeks red. She waits for her daddy's truck to drive through the black gate. She looks for hours down the country road. She waits day after day. She writes them letters at home, struggling with her yellow pencil on a piece of white paper with blue lines. Practicing every day, she writes in block letters that tumble over the line.

"Daddy, please come in your truck. Please pick me up. Please drive me home. The white fence along the country road must be on your way to somewhere. You must drive by one day. You'll see me on the white fence. I wave to you. You pick me up. You take me home."

Her daddy never comes. They never get her messages at home. The teachers keep the letters in their drawers in the cabinet at the far end of the classroom. Her mother and father don't get the hair she sends them, and Pia doesn't know that they don't get her pleas until she goes home for Christmas, when her parents tell her that they never received a word she wrote.

Sweet home. Sweet Mommy. Sweet Daddy. Sweet brother. She is home again. She'll never leave home again. Pia knows that there is no God in heaven. There is only home. That's that.

CHAPTER 3

Two days ago, Caron tells me that she is expecting. Expecting what? Oh, a baby? Yes, a baby and a baby. Two babies? I'm in the kitchen in the San Fernando Valley south of the Boulevard. I speak to her on the black phone that hangs on the wall above the cart that holds the small white television set on the top shelf. Last week's newspapers are piled high on the glass shelf below.

"That's not possible, Caron," I say to her in my too loud voice. "You are too small. We don't have twins in the family. Nice girls don't have twins. You must have taken one of those hormone pills." I say something close to that.

"No, Mom. They are fraternal. The doctor says that there must be twins somewhere on your side of the family."

"Is that so?" I try to mock her. "I believe you're mistaken. You say you dropped two eggs? What does that mean? Eggs? I've never heard of such a thing. No, sir. Never. Never have I heard such a thing."

"Don't be such a queen," Caron laughs at me.

"Eggs?" I repeat. "Could you please not be so specific? I don't want to hear about eggs. We don't cackle our lives away in this family. We are a nice family."

Oh, my God. Yesterday, I was young and beautiful. Today, I'm old and ugly. Today, I'm a grandmother of two. Please, dear God. Don't let them be boys. Two boys. They cannot come to visit. No, we will meet at McDonald's once a week. I will buy them each a Happy Meal. They may have all the French fries in the world they want.

They may fill their stomachs with Coca-Cola, for all I care. Be my guests. They will always remember me as their nice grandma. Their other grandma will feed them broccoli and spinach. They will hate her. They won't even attend her funeral. They will not attend her funeral.

They must not crawl all over the furniture. They must not crawl on the walls. They must not crawl on the ceiling. And they are not allowed to have toy guns. They must not fart in public. They must never laugh while they fart. I can't stand it. I am going back to my king-size bed. I shall be living a Proust novel in my old age. I shall eat madeleines and drink tea. I shall be quiet and sickly. No, they cannot visit their grandma today. She is not feeling well. Their grandmother is not well today. She is never feeling well again. She is going to die soon.

How could Caron do this to me? How could she? From the day she was born with her head turned around at Swedish Hospital in Seattle, she was a pain. She was a pain from the day she looked up at me with her blue eyes. Without a sign of guilt, she looked up at me after just having ruptured my uterus like a red balloon. Twenty-two hours of hard labor, and that's the thanks I get. Two boys. Two.

They better know the truth from the beginning. Their mother was a pain. Of course, she has to have two. No, she is never ordinary, their mother isn't. Caron was an impossible baby. It's a fact. She screamed for three months. She screamed for three months without stopping. She screamed till she turned blue in the face.

She shattered the windows. She shattered my spirit. Yes, their mother was a screamer. You could hear her all the way down the hill on Eleventh Street on Queen Anne Hill in Seattle. The street was littered with glass. You could hear her scream above the rooster's crowing across the street. You could hear her scream across Puget Sound all the way up to the Canadian border.

My God, the twins are going to be funny looking. Of course, they will weigh in at about three pounds each, with luck. They will be two scrawny monkeys with tiny baby blue caps. They better live even though they are monkeys. They better not break their mother's heart. They better grow up. They better do something with their lives or I will smack their little monkey bottoms.

I'll tell them as soon as they are born: "Do something with your lives, for God's sake. Do something. Don't just lie there in your baby blue caps thinking that acting cute is enough in this world. Grow up. Be doctors. Be lawyers. Be the president. Be anything but yourselves. Don't be monkeys, for God's sake."

As if I care. I hear that they train monkeys in Thailand to pick coconuts off the trees. They say that a human can pick only about a hundred coconuts a day. A monkey, on the other hand, can pick at least five hundred. So there. The twins may pick five hundred coconuts a day for the rest of their lives. What do I care? They may do what they want for the rest of their lives.

Caron always did what she wanted. She screamed, and she screamed some more. Her face turned blue. Caron weighed in at a normal seven pounds at birth. Her head was covered in soft blond fuzz, and the biggest, bluest eyes stared up at me. They are green now, her eyes are. They are the color of green apples. They are like mine used to be before they faded away.

Caron stared up at me, and she screamed her little head off while I stood in the middle of the room. I didn't want to throw her out of the window. I didn't want to throw myself out of the window. I wanted to throw myself out of the window with her in my arms. I stood far away from the window.

Caron doesn't show much gratitude on the phone when I remind her that I didn't throw her out the window. Instead, she blames me for the twins. That's the thanks I get. Caron must know how close she came not to grow up to become the mother she's going to be soon. Only my selfless love saved her.

I remind her that only some deep motherly instinct saved her when I wanted to put a pillow over her mouth to muffle her wailing. Please, someone, make her stop screaming, I prayed while I stood far away from the windows in the living room. I prayed, looking down in mortal fear at her small body in my arms, that I would be able to find enough food to feed her. My God, she will stay tiny in my arms forever. I am not capable of taking care of her, I cried to myself.

My heart was sinking then. It sank to the bottom of the basement and crashed against the cement floor next to the heater. It shattered into a million pieces. I picked up the pieces and glued them back together. They looked like a heart again. I put the new-fashioned object back into the hole gaping at the world on my left side—and the heart sat beating again.

I fed her from my breasts. Yes, the twin's ugly old granny has breasts. They were beautiful before Caron drank and sucked the life out of them. Now, thirty-two years later, their grandmother's breasts look like two sunken fried eggs. They are disgusting. I'm disgusting. Eggs. Eggs, all over the place. I'm disgusted.

Caron is big today, in a manner of speaking. She is five-foot-three. She weighs a little over a hundred pounds. How in the world will she carry twins? How will she do it? She is old now.

She is over thirty. The twins will know one day what it means to be over thirty. I will be dead by then.

The twins will tell their friends that they loved their grandmother. "We loved her to death," they'll tell them. "She was a hoot. She brought us up. She gave us comfort when our mother screamed at us. Grandma always took our side. She was the best of grandmothers. She was the best in the world."

Caron calls me on the phone. The doctor says they look perfect in there. Equal size, feet to feet they lie in her belly. She has gained five pounds. I tell her I am excited. I don't tell her I'm scared to death. "Please, don't kill her," I beg the twins in her womb.

A while ago Caron mentioned that she liked the name Wolfie for a boy. I hear myself asking her, "You're not planning to give them dog names like Wolfie and Rolfie, are you? No dog names, please. Please, they are boys. They are not dogs in there."

Caron says she'll move to Nepal if the twins are boys. She doesn't care if they're dogs if they are boys. She'll leave them in Los Angeles with their father if they're boys. She will leave them. The twins should know that she will leave them with their father. She is no saint. I'm no saint, either. I'm taking off for Nepal, too. I'll stay young in Katmandu. I'll chant. I'll become a high priestess. No granny, me.

The twins' father, resembling a scared orphan, says it is time to grow up and get a job. He should have thought about that a long time ago. He should have thought about that before spreading his seed across the world. I tell him that I love him. I have to tell him that I love him now that he is the father of my grandchildren. I ask myself what kind of father he'll make. Oh, my God. Their father better not be a loser. I'll smack him.

I tell Caron that I can't wait to see her. I will see her next Sunday, and I will look at her swollen tummy. Must I also look at the huge tattoo that stretches across her belly as far as the eye can see? Her body is mine. She knows that she comes from my loins. I can't stand the thought of her tattooed stomach. I can't wait to see her stomach.

The twins will stop her in her tracks. She doesn't know it yet. How can she know it? They'll stop her midway on her journey in life. I'm pissed, pissed, pissed. Yes, their nice grandmother talks like that when she is pissed. Their grandmother is pissed. She is hip, and she is cool. She is their fun grandmother.

I read today on the second page of the *Los Angeles Times* that the Chinese government is on a campaign to get men to cover up their bodies in the fine city of Beijing. The government wants to train their male citizens to have better manners for the upcoming Olympic Games in 2008. The government is getting ready for China to show a good face to the oncoming hordes of well-behaved Europeans and Americans.

I'm sure the Chinese government would prefer it if all the men and boys of China stayed inside in front of the television set forever. I ask myself at the breakfast table if five years would be time enough for the daunting task of cleaning up the act of male creatures anywhere in the world. Would five years of concerted effort finally stop all the fat guts from rolling over the pants in public? Would it stop the farting, the swearing, and the picking of noses in public? And how about stopping men from spitting like a bunch of llamas?

What's the matter with them, anyway? Why do boys always have to show off? I tell the twins this in advance: "You may go to your rooms. You may waste your life away for all I care as long as you stay inside on the couch watching television. And how about wearing a shirt to the dinner table? How about taking off your baseball caps?"

I'm going back to my king-size bed now to drown my sorrow. Oh, two boys. No, I'll go to Loehmann's instead. I'll go shopping with their aunt, who is only nineteen. How can they do this to Suzanna: making her an aunt of two at the age of nineteen? It's not fair. We'll shop. Shopping will make us forget our trials.

I'd better lose ten pounds before the twins see the light. Their grandmother is sexy. She is young. Ten pounds by February. I can do it. I'll starve myself. They'll be proud of their grandmother when they enter this world under the sign of Aquarius.

I don't believe that we are doomed in advance by the stars. I don't believe in silly stuff like that. It's nonsense. I look up their sign in the astrological forecast dreamed up by Sydney Omarr in the *Los Angeles Times*: February-Aquarius. Aquarius-February. I read what it means today to be born under the sign of Aquarius: "Asking price for property is inflated. Hold your ground; you get your way tonight. Highlight versatility and humor; what you feared will be a laughing matter."

A laughing matter. Sydney Omarr certainly has a way with words. I've read somewhere that he changed the *i* to *y* in his first name and assumed Omarr ending with double *r* as his last name to harmonize with the numerological spheres. With an ear for a melodic cadence and a nose for stardom, the down-to-earth Sidney Kimmelman transmuted at a young age into the heavenly Sydney Omarr. Knowing better than anyone what's in a name, Omarr would surely be able to see the difference between the Pia of my youth and the Pea that I have become. He also makes this little disclaimer at the bottom of his column: "The astrological forecast should be read for entertainment."

I remind myself that I read the twins' future sign for a good laugh and not in any way to have the upper hand. I also read that they, being born in the year of the Chinese Horse, are naturally popular and attractive to the opposite sex. They are often ostentatious and impatient. They need people. Marry a Tiger or a Dog early, but never a Rat.

I married a Tiger before I knew that the Tiger was a good match for me. Jeffrey is a Tiger. I am a Dog. A Tiger should look for happiness to the Dog and the Horse. He should look out for Monkeys. The Tiger is aggressive and courageous. He is also sensitive and candid. I thank my lucky stars that Jeffrey and I are made for each other. How lucky can you be marrying your perfect match without even knowing it?

Caron, Suzanna, and I, we are all Dogs. Loyal and honest, we work well with others. We are generous, yet stubborn and often selfish. We should look to the Horse or the Tiger, and we must always watch out for Dragons.

It's surely easier to spot a Rat than a Dragon. It's no laughing matter to have to look for Dragons. They are not easy to spot hiding behind whatnot. I, on the other hand, am easy to spot. I'm a Rat's Rat.

The signs trick you. I'm no Dog. I don't kiss ass. The stars are treacherous. I'm no virgin with the lamp. The twins will be right to say after they are born: "We don't know her. She is not really our grandmother." A Rat is ambitious yet honest and prone to spending freely. So there. I'm clearly a Rat. It's clear as day: I'm a Rat.

CHAPTER 4

Isee the child again in the black-and-white photograph. She stands next to her Cousin Gudrun beneath the naked branches of the trees. She holds her gray coat out at the hem while she fans the lower corner out with her left hand. The second button from the top is not closed. Her blond bangs fall below the knitted hat, and she smiles at the camera as she tilts her head a little to the side.

Pia tries on the gray coat. She likes herself in front of the dressing room mirror. She begs her mommy to buy her the gray coat. She cannot live without the coat. She will die if she doesn't get it. She looks at her mother with a shy little smile, tilting her head to the side. "Please, Mommy, let me have it," she begs. "I'll be good."

Agreeing to pay five crowns a month, her mother buys the coat for her on credit. For years to come her mother is in debt to Bolette Department Store, which stands five stories high on Kultorvet Square in the center of Copenhagen. Her mother can't afford the coat, but she can't deny her daughter anything she wants.

On this late afternoon in the fall, Pia is the fancy princess of Princess Street School. She is the princess who stands in her new gray coat in the classroom observing the blue ink stains on her desk with the two sunken inkwells placed into round holes cut out at equal distance from the middle. The cold coal stove rises tall and black behind her in the back of the classroom next to the three big windows that face Princess Street. She looks down at the blue stains on her fingers, and she walks out the door in her gray coat.

17

She leaves behind the room where in the morning Willy had smiled at her with his teeth rotted down to small brown stubs. Celebrating his birthday today, Willy had brought to school thirty-six creamy caramels wrapped in paper, one for each of his classmates. Willy has no winter coat, and his face and his hair have not seen water and soap since the day he was born. But it's his birthday today, and his mother has bought him caramels to share with his friends.

Dressed in his everyday brown pants falling short over his sockless feet in the worn shoes open without their shoelaces, Willy begins handing out the caramels from the back of the room. He walks the three rows from seat to seat. The classmates, thinking that the candy is dirty, won't take a piece from his bag. Not even Rosa, who has not seen a creamy caramel in weeks, will take a piece of his candy.

Sitting way up in front of the classroom, Pia is the last to be offered one of the caramels. Unable to hear the teacher clearly with her ears closed shut by the eczema, she always sits face-to-face with the teacher. She looks down at the thirty-six pieces of candy, and she sees Willy's blue eyes peering scared and sad over the brown paper bag. She takes a caramel and says, "Thank you. Happy birthday, Willy." He smiles at her. Willy's smile glows on Princess Street.

It's late in the afternoon. Dressed like a princess in her gray coat, she leaves the classroom behind. It is gray and damp outside. The air feels thick. She sees the gray cement yard where the classes line up in two rows of eighteen each in the morning. She sees the yard where they stand straight like little tin soldiers with their brown schoolbags in hand at 8:00 a.m. sharp, six days a week. Mr. Nielsen hits them on the back of the head if he sees them step out of line. That's his job. Fifty years from now the building lies in rubble after being demolished for a new building. It's a big black hole.

She walks out onto the street and heads home from Princess Street School in Christianshavn to number 8B on Queen's Street. She lives in the oldest and poorest part of Copenhagen. She lives in Christianshavn long before it becomes a charming, upscale area with no drunkards lurking in the dark corners of the streets.

She walks down Princess Street in her gray coat. She sees Our Savior's Church on her right a little behind her. Worming its way up into the gray sky, the tall tower drills like a green corkscrew up into a big gold ball balanced on the tip. She feels cozy and warm. The gray belt closes snugly in a fake bone buckle around her waist.

She turns right on Torve Street and comes to the big square. She sees the round kiosk to the left where every day her daddy buys his newspapers and his cigarettes. She sees two brown statues, one of a seated Eskimo woman and one of a kayak that, moored high on its column, cuts like a knife through the air.

She walks past the entrance to the library where she sits in the evening on the little chair at the low round table in the children's room. She likes the warm smell of the library. She cannot read the words quite easily yet, but she likes looking at the pictures in the books.

Pia likes the pictures in the story of "The Princess and the Pea" best of all. She likes it when the princess sticks her legs way up in the air. She laughs out loud when the princess loses her balance on top of the high pile of the twenty mattresses and the twenty goose-down pillows. The pea is so small that neither Pia nor the princess can see it with the naked eye. But Pia knows it is hidden way under the mattresses and the pillows. She sees that the princess is in terrible pain. Pia sees that she is the real princess.

She walks along the square past the library. She sees the movie theater across the square where she watches movies on Sundays. Pia loves Sundays. It's the best day in the whole week. Each Sunday, her mommy gives her little brother and her two quarters to share, one quarter for a twin popsicle and one for the movies.

Poul and Pia buy the popsicle in the candy store on the left side of Queen's Street close to the square on their way to the theater. Pia breaks it in two. Her brother likes the green part. She likes the red.

The man at the theater lets them share a seat for the other quarter. They squeeze into the seat. Poul wiggles around. He can't sit still. Pia punches him on the arm. They watch Laurel and Hardy on the screen. They watch Charlie Chaplin. She doesn't think that Charlie Chaplin is as funny as Laurel and Hardy. She laughs out loud when the window drops down on Laurel's head.

When Pia, in her gray coat, reaches the far corner of the square, the yellow streetcar number two cranks across the crosswalk on Torve Street. She stops for the red light. The light turns green, and she walks across the crosswalk. She turns right toward the canal.

She walks down to Over Street along the canal and looks to her right. She sees the short tower of Christiana Church behind the buildings that line the other side of the canal. She steps up on the one-foot high wooden barrier that guards the canal. The wood is wet and mossy with slime.

She takes careful steps with her brown schoolbag in her right hand. She holds her right arm out straight to the side for balance. The schoolbag dangles over the canal. Her left arm is straight out over the cobblestone street. She puts one foot in front of the other. It's fun. She can do it.

Squoosh. Her right foot slides to the right just a little. She feels the butter under her feet. She is in the air. It takes no time whatsoever to drop ten feet to the surface of the oily green water. It takes no time at all to drop to the bottom like a stone.

She is deep down in the canal. It's silent. She pops up like a cork. Stretching her arms up into the air, she uses her right hand to grab onto the twisted rope that holds a small boat tethered to the side of the canal. She is quiet. She looks up at the side of the boat in front of her. Dark blue paint peels off the rotting wood of the boat.

She looks over her right shoulder. She sees a red boat behind her. With more than half her body plunged in the canal, she hangs suspended between two boats. She is little. She cannot swim. She sees her brown bag floating away behind her on the green water toward the square with the statue of the Eskimo woman. It washes away like a lonely piece of brown wood that bobs up and down in the oily canal.

Hanging like a gray rag doll in her wet furry coat, the child holds on with her hands tight around the rope. She doesn't make a sound. Around the curved side of the blue boat, she sees two men rowing toward her. They look big in the small boat. She hears the oars hit the water. The boat reaches her. The bigger of the two men plucks her up out of the water and pulls her into the boat. He is Popeye the Sailor Man. She has seen him before on the screen from her seat in the theater. A green-and-red anchor shows on his right upper arm below his rolled up red-and-black checkered shirtsleeve.

The sailor man carries her up the iron stairs attached to the wall from the surface of the water of the canal. Holding onto the stairs with his left arm, he carries her in his right arm up to the street. She feels lighter than spring air in his arm. They are up. He is silent. They stand, the two of them together on the cobblestone street. Water drips from the bottom of her gray coat.

They see the other man still in the boat rowing toward her brown schoolbag that floats away on top of the oily green water. He scoops it out of the canal with his right hand and rows back to the staircase. He walks up the stairs and hands her the brown schoolbag. She lifts it up by the handle with her right hand. Two small waterfalls rush from the sides of the bag down onto the cobblestones below her boots. He says, "Go home to your mother. Go home."

CHAPTER 5

The child turns to her right, making sure to stay away from the edge of the canal. In her wet coat, she drags her feet in the middle of the street. She lifts her boots warily over the golden brown dung left by two large horses that pull the Carlsberg beer housed in wooden crates on the flat cart behind them.

Around the corner, she passes the saloon. Glancing in, she sees a woman slumped over the table in the back of the room. She sees the purple lipstick smeared around the woman's wide mouth and the brown hair falling in big clumps around her face. Pia smells stale beer and old vomit.

She reaches Queen's Street. She lifts her wet boots across the legs that stretch bandaged in dirty old rags over the cobblestones. Using the wall for a pillow, the drunkard lies on the street with his head against the building. His swollen cheeks shine red behind the black grease.

She sees the bakery across the street where she rummages through the day-old rolls before they are thrown out with the garbage in the morning. She sees the baker who lets her bring home the leftover rolls to her mother for morning coffee.

She walks past the greengrocer's shop. She doesn't want the greengrocer to notice her. Yesterday, her teacher, Mrs. Pedersen, made her go into his shop to say she was sorry. "I'm so sorry," Pia had whispered when the class had been on its way to feed the white swans that nest by the lake in Volden's Park bordering the end of Queen's Street. Now Pia hopes that the greengrocer won't see her because she doesn't want to remind him of the crime she had committed yesterday morning when the class was on a school outing.

Today, seeing the shop, Pia is forced to relive the shameful event when, two by two, she and one of her classmates had walked holding hands in back of the class. Passing by the greengrocer's shop, she had seen the green leeks, the orange carrots, the red apples, and the brown onions in the wooden crates neatly placed on the sidewalk. She had picked up two onions from their crate and pushed them in under her blouse, placing them on her chest. She jumped around like a clown. The two onions bounced up and down under her blouse. She thought she looked like Mrs. Pedersen. She was sure she had grown a bosom like Mrs. Pedersen's. She laughed. Her friends laughed. Mrs. Pedersen looked at her. "What's that?"

"What's that?" Mrs. Pedersen asked again in a stern voice.

"It's nothing," Pia answered, trying to hide the fear in her laughing eyes.

"Take them out, you silly girl," Mrs. Pedersen snapped at her while she pulled her by the ear into the greengrocer's shop.

With her ear pulled low to one side, Pia saw the greengrocer in his brown apron looking short behind the counter. She handed him the two onions. She curtsied and whispered, "I'm sorry." He glanced down at the two onions, and then he gazed at her through his round thick glasses, not knowing what to say.

Today, walking past the greengrocer's shop in her wet coat, she stares hard down at the cement squares that make even lines in the sidewalk. "Don't walk on the lines," her friends tell her. "If you walk on the black line, you will kiss a Negro." The only Negro she has ever seen is in *Little Black Sambo* at the library.

She thinks that Sambo looks quite sweet with his green umbrella and the red top that hangs loose over his blue pedal pushers ending just below his knees. But why risk it? Lifting her wet boot across the line, Pia is not inclined to take a chance on ever kissing a Negro.

She walks past the basement grocery shop where she buys licorice drops when she has ten cents in her pocket. The lady grocer, with the mustache growing dark on her upper lip, rolls a small piece of white paper into the shape of a cone before she counts out ten pieces and drops them into the cone one at a time. Pia no longer buys the chocolate frogs filled with a thick white cream.

She hears from her friends on the street that you can grow a baby in your stomach from eating a frog. Pia will not eat a frog again. Though she has not yet heard that you shouldn't eat anything living in water without fins and scales, she knows at an early age to stay away from frogs.

She walks past the coal man who lives in the basement next to the grocer. He is the keeper of the mountain of black coal. Pia fills her bucket from the mountain whenever her mother needs her to go down to fetch some coal. When her mother asks her, she carries the bucket down the street to the coal man, who shovels the coal up to the rim. She drags the heavy bucket back to number 8B and up the stairs to her mommy.

She sees a few pieces of coal on the street as she walks in her wet coat past the coal man to number 8B on Queen's Street. She turns left up the worn stone stairs to the black door. She sees 8B printed in white upon the small blue square tacked high on top of the black door. She opens the door and walks into the brown hallway. She sees the dim lightbulb that dangles on its cord from the ceiling.

She sees the door on her right. Mrs. Hansen, with the blue-and-white porcelain flowerpots in her window, lives behind it. Pia walks up the wooden stairs that rise steep in the back of the hallway. The steps curve thin in the middle from wear. She smells the cabbage and the fried onions. The wet gray coat pulls her down as she walks up the stairs. She holds on tight to the wood railing.

She walks up to the first floor and sees to the left of her the first door. Behind it lives Mr. Olsen alone with his fish tank. Pia and her little brother visit him often in his apartment. They like to look at the fish swimming in his tank. Her brother likes the blue one, and she likes the yellow one with the black stripes. Mr. Olsen likes her brother more than he likes her.

Her brother is four. He goes over to Mr. Olsen's apartment to watch the fish as much as he likes. He is always welcome. She hears her mother whisper to her father, "Egon, do you think it's a good idea that Poul spends so much time alone with Mr. Olsen?" Her mother doesn't want Pia to hear them speaking. But she hears. "Don't worry," Egon says to Putte in a mocking voice.

"Don't worry so much," she hears her daddy answering her mommy. Pia worries like her mommy. Like her mommy she knows there are signs out there. Always look for the signs. Don't break the mirror or your luck will run out. Don't walk on the black line. Don't face away from the door. Don't let a black cat cross your path. Don't put your shoes on the table. Don't eat a frog. Don't walk under a ladder. Don't ever steal onions or your luck will run out.

She sees the door next to hers just a ways down the hallway. Behind it live Mia and Rikke with their mom and dad in the apartment right above Mrs. Hansen with the blue-and-white flowerpots in the window. Mia and Rikke's dad smacks his wife around in their apartment. They all hear the banging through the wall.

Mia and Rikke's mommy is pretty when her blue eyes aren't black. She makes pretty drawings with crayon pencils on nice velvety paper. Mia and Rikke's mommy gives Pia a drawing of a pretty lady with pretty eyelashes shading the eyes.

Pia keeps the drawing next to her box of crayons and her rubber doll named Heidi. She keeps it in her own drawer in the bottom of the dresser before she gives it to Uncle Thor as a present. She tells her uncle that she drew it herself. Believing her, he puts it in his big book about the family. "My niece has talent," Uncle Thor says proudly.

She hears her mommy whisper to her daddy, "Please, go over there. Make him stop. He's going to kill her." Pia hears them whisper in the corner on the brown divan. She is awake, and she is afraid that Mia and Rikke's mommy will die when the dad beats her. Pia's daddy is big and brave. He stomps next door in his white long johns that cover the scars on his white legs. He bangs on the door.

They hear loud yelling in number 8B. The noise comes through their door from the hallway. The door down the hallway bangs shut. It's quiet. Her daddy comes back. He crawls back on the divan next to her mommy. They go back to sleep.

Standing in her wet coat, she sees the door across from Mia and Rikke's door. Mr. Petersen used to live behind that door once. Now, he is away in prison because he did something naughty to Mia and Rikke. His young wife, blond and tall, now lives alone across from Mia and Rikke.

The young Mrs. Petersen is the daughter of Mrs. Jensen, the fat old landlady who lives below Mr. Olsen and his fish tank. Her mommy tells Pia in secret that the landlady's daughter is slow in her thinking. "She is not quite with it," her mommy tells her, shaking her head a little.

Pia is also told that the fat landlady had at one time been married to Mr. Petersen. That was before the landlady came home and found her husband in bed with her daughter, who then became the new Mrs. Petersen. The daughter now lives alone on the floor above her old mother, who calls herself Mrs. Jensen again. Two or three more families live above all of them on the third floor under the roof.

Pia knocks on the door to her right across from Mr. Olsen's door. She knocks on the door again. She stands in her gray coat in a pool of water and waits for her mommy to open the door.

CHAPTER 6

The mother looks down at her young daughter's brown boots soaked in a pool of water, and her hazel eyes grow big behind the glasses. She sees the water seeping out between the soles and the brown leather of the boots. She looks up and notices the oil spreading across the front of the gray coat in big black blotches.

Her mother, with one hand up over her mouth, pulls Pia from the hallway into the kitchen. Pia sees her little brother in the alcove with his legs crossed on the mattress, eating a piece of pumpernickel bread. The white sugar shimmers on top of the yellow butter.

Pia feels her mother's hand shaking as it opens her belt and unbuttons the gray coat. She feels her mother's hand pulling her arms out of the wet sleeves. The coat looks heavy in her mother's hand. Pia smells rotten fish and oil. She doesn't know where her mother hangs the gray coat.

Her mother strips her naked and puts a kettle of water on the gas burner that stands alone attached to a red rubber hose coming out of the wall above the concrete table across from the sink. Her mother lifts her up on the counter next to the sink and dries her face with the washcloth. The kettle begins to whistle.

Her mother takes the kettle off the burner and pours water into a shallow metal basin in the sink. She puts a little cold water into the hot water and places her daughter's feet into the basin. She takes the washcloth in her right hand and circles it around her daughter's hair and face. The washcloth turns black.

Pia smells the green Palmolive soap when her mommy washes her neck. Her mother pours out the black soapy water and fills the basin with warm water again. She rinses the washcloth out in the cold water from the faucet and dips the cloth into the warm water. She rinses off her daughter's hair and face. She rinses her body and legs before drying her off with the white towel.

Pia's naked body shivers pink as a newborn baby on the counter. Her mommy dresses her in the blue-with-white dotted pajamas. Pia has to pee.

Her mommy lets her pee in the sink tonight. Pia does not have to walk across the back courtyard in the dark and cold air to the shed where the two rusted iron toilets stand missing their seats. She doesn't have to go down to the toilets shared by the sixteen families who live in 8B and 8A. Not tonight. She does not have to bring her roll of toilet paper down to the courtyard. She does not have to smell the urine and the shit. Her mommy washes her pee down the drain with cold water.

Pia smells the milk and chocolate boiling in the small blue pan on the burner. She walks into the living room with her cup of hot chocolate. The brown divan stands in the corner where her parents sleep at night. She sees the big brown stain on the wall left from where the rain seeps through the walls. The table with four chairs covered in yellow damask stands in the middle of the room.

It's the same table that moves with them to the postwar tenements on Sandhus Road number 25 in the suburb of Valby a few years later. She sees the two stuffed chairs, one standing in each corner below the paned glass windows with the beige cotton curtains.

The gray coat is hidden away. Pia, cozy in her blue-with-white dotted pajamas, sits at the table. Warm and pink, she drinks her hot chocolate. She sees the red glow of burning coal through the flower-patterned holes in the little door of the iron stove.

Her mother pushes the curry-colored chairs together, making them into a bed. She puts the white pillow on the end of the two chairs that stands closest to the stove. "Always face the door, or your luck will run out," her mommy tells her.

She crawls into bed, and her mommy tucks the white comforter around her. Pia is safe. Her mommy whispers to her, "Don't tell Daddy about the coat. You know that he has told you many times to stay away from the canal. Don't tell Daddy. We don't want to make him mad, do we? Don't tell Daddy. Go to sleep now before he comes home. Go to sleep."

The child goes to sleep. She is sleeping with her secret on the chairs covered in knobby velour the color of dirty curry. She sleeps safeguarded from all evil right on the spot where her father places the Christmas tree in the big pot every year.

On Christmas Eve, Poul and Pia decorate the tree with red paper hearts. They circle it with long chains of red and green paper. They sit on their father's lap. He then reads "The Little Match Girl" out loud to them from their grandfather's old leather-bound book.

Crying rivers of tears, Poul and Pia weep the loudest when their daddy comes to the part where the Little Match Girl burns her last match as she sits dying in the snow piled high on the cold street. They beg him to read it again. "Please, Daddy. Please, read it one more time, Daddy."

He reads it again. They sing: "High on the top of the green tree, shines the light of Christmas...." They sing with their eyes glued to the top of the tree, gazing at the white star that glitters in the light of the candles. They open the presents: a rubber doll for Pia. A red car for Poul. Their mother plays the small upright piano that stands against the back wall next to the coal stove.

No one else has a piano on Queen's Street. No one is as rich as they are. They are rich. They are special. They live in a castle. They see their mother's big hands moving across the keys, and they hear her sing, "Silent Night, Holy Night" in her beautiful high voice.

Her brother wears a red Christmas hat. A white cotton beard covers his chin like Santa Claus's. Pia wears a red hat also. Her brother bends his head over the tree's lit candle. The white cotton beard catches fire. Their mother grabs Pia, and the two of them run through the kitchen and out into the dark hallway. They see from the hallway Poul standing next to the Christmas tree with his beard in flames.

They see her father through the open door grabbing the melting cotton off her little brother's face and dropping the beard onto the floor. They see the flames shooting out of the floor. Her father stomps them till they are out. Her little brother stands in front of the tree trimmed with the red hearts and the garlands, gaping at the flattened ball of melted cotton that by now squirms like a tarred cat wrestling with a ghost on the floor. Poul's hazel eyes grow big.

They try to eat the duck stuffed with prunes and apples. They try to eat the stewed red cabbage, the candied potatoes, and the rice porridge with the whole almond hidden in the bowl. "Whoever finds the almond first gets the present of the marzipan pig," their daddy reminds them. They try to find the almond.

They try to eat, but they are tired. Her father joins the two stuffed chairs into the curry-colored bed. Her mother kisses her good night. Pia knows that her mommy loves her best of all. She sees it in her hazel eyes that her mother loves her more than anything in the whole world.

Pia knows in her heart that her mother will protect her from fires and shield her from her father's bad temper if she only keeps quiet. She also knows that little secrets are not the same as little lies. Her mommy never lies. Her mommy is an angel sent down from heaven to keep her safe. Her little brother goes to the kitchen to sleep on his mattress placed on the floor. Her parents go to their divan in the corner. She hears them whisper in the dark.

This autumnal evening, Pia is sleeping safely on her two chairs in her blue-with-white dotted pajamas. The heat of the chocolate has made her sink deep into her dreams. Her father has not yet come home. Dressed in his big black coat, he is walking in the dark down Queen's Street. Worn and shredded, his black coat has turned gray at the end of the sleeves and around the collar.

Her father steps over the drunkards who, burrowing into their hand-me-down coats tied together with ropes, try to keep warm in the corners of the buildings. The child sees the red faces of the drunkards shining through the black grease in her dreams. She is afraid of them. She smells shit and wood alcohol as she steps across their legs. Her mommy holds her hand. "There is nothing to be afraid of," her mommy tells her in her dreams. "There is nothing to be afraid of. They can't move anymore. They are too tired and cold to move."

"But what about the man who dragged Lisa into the dark hallway and pulled her pants down?" she asks her mommy. "What about Mr. Petersen, who took Mia and Rikke into his bed? What about Mr. Petersen, who took their clothes off before he went off to prison?"

"Don't talk to strangers," her mother says.

"But Mommy, Mr. Olsen gives me candy," she says. "Mr. Olsen smiles at me. He lets me look at his fish."

"Don't talk to strangers," her mommy answers her in her dreams.

When her father comes home in the night, her mother takes the black coat away from him, telling him that he needs a new one. Her mother informs him that it is time to buy another coat for himself at the Salvation Army down the street. She doesn't tell him that she has decided to have his old black coat lined with her daughter's shaggy gray coat.

The tailor says, "I can do it." Then evening after evening, the mother and Pia take the streetcar in the dark to the tailor's small room. They walk behind tall buildings through long black hallways to the place where he takes measurements of the coat under a dim lightbulb.

"It's finished. It's done," the tailor finally tells them. The mother puts the new coat on her little daughter. Pia's arms, unable to move up or down, stick out like the two stuffed sleeves on the scarecrow standing guard in the middle of the wheat field.

"That will do," says her mommy, pleased with herself. She looks happy that her daughter has a warm coat again. Each month she pays the five crowns owed on credit to Bolette Department Store while her little girl waddles down the street looking like a pregnant black duck. The sleeves grow short over the child's bare wrists before her mother sells the black coat lined with the gray coat to the ragman standing in the court- yard below their windows.

Pia sees the ragman. He stands in front of the row of wooden sheds where the yellow-eyed street cats keep their kittens safe in the dark corners behind the twisted wheels and the wooden crates filled with nails and hammers and empty paint cans. "Rags, rags," he yells.

Pia sees him dressed in brown rags not too far from the shed where the two rusted toilets stand. His black shoes stretch long like the shoes that Charlie Chaplin wears on the big screen in the theater on the square. The ragman holds a brown burlap sack in his right hand. They hear him through the window from the courtyard on Queen's Street. They hear him.

Her father never knows that her gray coat lines his black coat. He dies, and he doesn't know that the ragman has the coat. They tell him nothing. Nothing at all.

Pia dreams of the drunkards on the street. While her father walks home alone in the night, she dreams in the two chairs made into a bed. He has been out looking for work again. No work today. He stops at the bar on his way home. Just a few beers. Why not? No work today.

And why should he not have a beer? Today, when that little Pia, who slept on the chairs with her secrets, is soon to be a granny, I struggle to lift the heavy curtain that hides the past. Holding in my hand a faded photograph of my father and me, I bend low to take a peek in under the hem at the scenes played out on the stage of life. Arm in arm, my father and I stand in front of a gaping hole where the building with numbers 8B and 8A used to present its plain but solid façade to the street before it burned down to the ground fifteen years after we lived in 8B.

Trying to find the signs that point backward to a time more distant yet than the moment captured after the fire, I can't stop staring at the photograph. I see myself posing for the camera with my left arm hooked through my father's right arm. I wear a short brown wool coat over a miniskirt woven in a brown-and-beige zigzag pattern. Brown leather boots reach up to my knees. My blond hair is cut short, with bangs that fall heavy over my eyebrows. Dressed in his gray suit and white shirt, my father lives on fixed deep in the emulsion of this faded color photograph casually snapped by Jeffrey three years into our marriage.

I'm mesmerized by the remains in my hand. I see in the photograph that I'm now fast traveling toward the age of my father as reflected in the tired lines on his face. Looking backward and still more afar, I glean from the gaze of our eyes that my father and I both, at that very moment in time, recalled the days when the building where we lived with my mother and brother in number 8B was still harboring us and the neighbors on Queen's Street. Although our features fade into the gap behind us, I'm able to see that we took pains to smile at the camera.

CHAPTER 7

Her father's blue eyes are the color of steel except when he drinks. After a few rounds of beers, the blue always turns to green. It is no laughing matter when the child sees the eye of the Dragon. But funnily enough, it is all too easy to laugh at Pia, who sees the green eye as merely another warning sign in her daily life: green eyes and your luck will run out.

Every day when her father comes home from work in his gray uniform, Pia runs to greet him on the street, checking out the color of his eyes. Then she flies home faster than the wind to her mother. Her job in the world is to prepare her mother for the level of intensity of the color green, the true measure of his state of drunkenness. She bounces up and down like a loose ball, yelling, "His eyes are green. His eyes are very very green."

Pia is pleased to do her job well. She thinks it lucky that no one picked up her father on his day of birth for an early funeral. He weighed thirteen pounds at birth. His mother, believing her newborn baby boy was dead, put him on the bare bench in the front room where he waited stark naked for someone to pick him up for his burial.

An hour later, he opened his eyes and began bellowing like a thirteen-pound seal. His huge head dangled off a solid weight of fat, and two skinny legs stuck out from his round body. "Egon is alive," they said in awe at the wonder of it all.

According to the story that Pia is told, even Egon's own mother, Hilda, had seemed more surprised than happy at her son's revival. Hilda was born sometime around the American Civil War, as were Pia's other three grandparents. "Where is there a war?" her grandparents would probably have asked.

Pia is certain that they never gave a thought to the Civil War and that they knew nothing of slaves. She doubts they ever saw a black person in their lives. "A black man? Who is black?" they would have queried one another, looking puzzled. "Abraham who? Who's Abraham Lincoln?"

Three of her grandparents died sometime in the 1930's. Only Hilda, Egon's unhappy mother, lived long enough to die in 1949, three years after Pia's birth. Hilda bore six children and gave each a name that began with E: Eleanor, Edy, Egor, Else, Egon, and Erik.

According to family gossip, Egon's sister, born twenty-five years before Pia's father, grew up to become a bad wife and a mean mother like Hilda had been. Aunt Eleanor married an engineer and moved into a nice rowhouse with a garden in Kastrup. Aunt Eleanor had only one son, named Willy. She pulled Willy's ears so much and so hard that they got big enough that he flew out of the house all by himself. "Your cousin can fly. He can fly," Egon tells his young daughter. She believes her father.

Aunt Edy, Hilda's second child, became a diabetic early in life. Pia doesn't ever see Aunt Edy with her real legs. She sees her always sitting in her wheelchair with only two black wooden stumps that stick straight out in the air.

Aunt Edy takes her wooden stumps on and off during the first visit that Pia remembers making to her aunt's house when she is around four. Aunt Edy lives on the fourth floor of a big apartment complex. Her mother and her aunt drink coffee and eat butter cookies. Her mother lets her go down to play in the backyard by herself.

Pia sits on the swing by herself for half an hour or so. Then she is finished with swinging and wants to go back up to her mommy, but she can't find her aunt's place on the fourth floor. Pia doesn't know where she is.

The child is lost. She runs up and down the stairs. She pants. She can't breathe. All the doors look the same. She peeks through the letter slots in the doors. "Please, is my mommy behind the door?" she prays. "Where is my mommy?"

She turns up the cover on the slot in the door with her right hand. Peeping in through the narrow slot, she sees a lady at the same moment as the lady sees two blue eyes staring in at her from the other side of the door. The lady opens the door and takes her into the apartment, where she puts the child up on her kitchen counter. The nice lady feeds her strawberries and milk. Pia eats strawberries while she cries for her mommy. She wants her mommy. She swallows her breath. She hiccups.

The words come out in huge gulps, "I want my mommy." The nice lady and the child look at each other. Pia doesn't see the nice lady call anyone. But she hears a knock on the door, and she sees men in dark blue uniforms walk into the kitchen. They pick her up and carry her to their black car, and they drive her away. She smells the diesel gasoline in the backseat of the car. She feels sick to her stomach.

They take her to the station, where she is fed chocolate pretzels. She eats the pretzels even though she misses her mommy. Pia loves the taste of milk chocolate. She can't say no to the chocolate even while she thinks she is going to die without her mommy. The child cries until she falls asleep under a desk.

The child wakes. She sees her mommy flying in through the door. She sees her mother red in the face. Her mother's hazel eyes look pink and swollen behind the glasses. Her mommy grabs her in her arms, and the child puts her head onto her mommy's warm breasts. She snuggles up and smells the familiar smell of sweet sweat. She smells her mommy. That's her memory of Aunt Edy.

Pia never meets Uncle Egor until Aunt Eleanor's funeral. He is a milkman. Seventeen then, Pia cries hard at Aunt Eleanor's funeral. She thinks it's horrible to die with so few tears, and she cries because she thinks it is horrible to die. No one cries at Aunt Eleanor's funeral but her. The husband doesn't cry. Willy, the son, doesn't cry. Pia looks at her cousin's ears. They are large. Her father is right: Aunt Eleanor was mean.

She also meets Uncle Kylle for the first time at Aunt Eleanor's funeral. Erik, nicknamed Kylle at an early age, is child number six. He is five years younger than Egon. In Danish, Kylle means a sort of small chicken.

Her grandmother had six children over a period of thirty years. "Kylle is a beautiful baby," everyone said. "He is her last," they prayed. Kylle got all the blond curls her father never got. Her father's head stayed bald as an egg until he was about five. It is bald again when he is thirty.

Pia's dad has no luck. Kylle gets all the luck in the world. He grows up to own a fashionable shoe shop in Copenhagen. He likes ladies' shoes better than men's. She hears he gives fun parties to which they are never invited.

Eighteen years older than Kylle and the youngest of the three sisters, Aunt Else grows up to become a kleptomaniac. But first, she becomes pregnant at the age of eighteen by some no-good scoundrel. A widower and a newspaper editor, her own uncle by marriage weds Aunt Else to save her good name when he is sixty-three.

Pia is told over and over again by her father that Aunt Else had always been madly in love with the uncle she marries when she is pregnant with her first son. "She loved him even when his wife was alive. She loved him always. Aunt Else and her uncle made a good marriage," her father tells her.

Pia is also told that Aunt Else and her new husband neglected their new baby boy named Poul just a little. Aunt Else was eighteen, and the uncle worked at the paper all day. "Poul was left in his crib alone when they went out to dinner," her father tells Pia when he talks to her about his sister.

Aunt Else and the uncle were married for about ten years before the uncle died. Aunt Else never married again after his death. She had a good pension from the newspaper. Though she wanted to remain unmarried, Aunt Else did have a second son with a waiter.

Pia does remember meeting the waiter once in the apartment in Valby. She remembers the aunt and the waiter sitting beside each other at the dining room table. Her mother feeds them meatballs with stewed white cabbage. Pia loves her mother's cooking. She eats the meatballs fried crisp and brown in butter and the cabbage stewed in white cream.

She couldn't be happier on this one evening, sitting across from her aunt and the waiter eating her mother's dinner. Their son, whom they named Morten, is now long grown, but it shows in the waiter's eyes that he is still in love with Aunt Else even though she has refused to marry him after all these years. It is clear that the waiter can't keep his hands off of her aunt's knees under the table.

In Pia's mind, the aunt and the waiter look too old across from her to cuddle over their meatballs. She is sure they are ancient since by now they look to be in their sixties. Her mother whispers to her, "Fire burns hot in old houses." Pia thinks about what her mother means by that comment while she eats her meatballs.

The family legend goes that Aunt Else takes her brother, the little chicken, out shopping to console herself in the years after her husband's death. She takes Kylle, just about fourteen years old then, along with her on her shopping sprees in the time between her husband's death and meeting the waiter.

Aunt Else and Kylle don't go shopping the normal way. They are not normal, either of them. They shop for fur coats without a dime to their names. Pia is not sure how they manage to do it. Pia is never quite told the details of their exploits. They are better left to the imagination, according to her father.

Pia imagines her aunt trying on the coat. She sees Kylle distracting the saleslady with his lovely long curls while her aunt sneaks out the door and waltzes down the street without a worry in the world. Kylle tries on his own black mink coat. "This one is lovely," he says as he smiles at himself in the mirror. His love for fur is clearly set at an early age.

The saleslady is smitten and flustered by Kylle's curls falling just above the black collar of the mink coat. "He's lovely," the saleslady thinks. Kylle and the saleslady are busy looking in the mirror while Aunt Else, dressed in the black coat that fits her perfectly, skips down the street. Her great legs show nicely in their silk stockings with the seams running up her calves, vanishing under the fur hem as sure and straight as her step strikes the sidewalk.

In the meantime, Aunt Edy, with the two wooden stumps for legs, doesn't move around her apartment much. She doesn't even know what's in her closet. She doesn't know what goes on around her. When the police finally open the door to Aunt Edy's closet, hundreds of fur coats fall out, tumbling to the floor in front of her chair.

Aunt Edy is shocked beyond words. She is speechless. The wooden legs stick straight up in the air. "I don't need a fur coat for my wooden legs," Aunt Edy whispers. "I never in my life needed a mink coat. I never go anywhere. I don't own a mink, ever. How? How did they get here?"

Aunt Else was not charged with a crime, and Kylle, due to his young age, was merely named an innocent accomplice. But the scandal was nevertheless published in the dead husband's newspaper. It was decided by a higher authority that Aunt Else suffered from despondency and a case of bad nerves. "She's in a deep depression," the doctors said. "It's a mental thing with her." Then Aunt Else was promptly sent away for a little while to recover her peace of mind in the sanitarium in the meadows.

Pia is told that Aunt Else's first son grew up to become a Catholic, and then he killed himself. She never meets her Cousin Poul. She knows you are not supposed to be a Catholic and kill yourself. No good Catholic kills himself. You burn in hell if you kill yourself if you are a Catholic. No one in the family has ever been a Catholic.

Pia knows that Cousin Poul never gets to see the kingdom of heaven even though he says his Hail Marys over and over again. She imagines him praying and stroking the string of beads of the Rosary through his long fingers. She sees him making the sign of the cross and reciting the Apostles' Creed.

He prays: "Our Father, which art in heaven, hallowed be

thy name; thy kingdom come; thy will be done, on earth as it is in heaven... For thine is the kingdom, and the power, and the glory, forever and ever. Amen."

Cousin Poul finishes with "Glory be to the Father." He repeats the last three steps for each decade of his life in a set of ten beads, and still he kills himself. Cousin Poul is brought to the hard testing, as it says in the Bible. He is not kept safe from the Evil One.

Pia thinks that it isn't fair that her Cousin Poul did not get to see the kingdom of heaven, considering how hard he prayed. It's too strange to see the hand of God striking with a twisted vengeance. She thinks that all those prayers that come to nothing in the end are useless blather.

She sees that whipping yourself and begging for mercy lead nowhere. Pray, for all she cares about it. Pray for a bicycle. Pray for gold. Pray for strawberry ice cream. Pray for a castle. Pray for a small nose. Pray for rain. Pray for a pair of new shoes. Pray for a long life. Pray till hell freezes over. There is no God in heaven.

Egon, the fifth child, grows up to be a truck driver. But before taking on that occupation, he spent time in a concentration camp in Germany. That is the story she is told in a whisper by her mother. Pia doesn't understand why her mother's voice sounds ashamed telling her this story.

The family never talks much about her father's time in Germany. She doesn't understand the silence. She would have liked to say out loud that her father was a man of conviction. "He is a man of conviction and not a man of bad luck," she wishes to say. Instead, Pia feels ashamed.

She is told that her father wrote some sort of letter during the war to a Danish friend who lived in Germany at the time. Somehow, it was intercepted before it crossed the border between Denmark and Germany. It might be said that in the scheme of things, her dad wrote a letter at the wrong time and in the wrong place. Her dad had no luck in life.

By the time her father wrote the letter, the Germans had crossed into Denmark, and they were now sitting in the Danish kitchens stuffing their faces with eggs and bacon. They were at the table spreading the creamy butter on their breakfast rolls. They looked out of the window upon the yellow wheat of Denmark. They gazed upon the Elysian Fields nestled gently in the golden sunlight and the blue breezes. They sat at the table ogling the bottomless breadbasket and the homemade strawberry jam.

Her father might have written a few unkind words about the Germans. Maybe he mentioned, only in a lighthearted manner, of course, "The Germans, they eat like pigs. The straps on their helmets are growing a bit tight around their rosy cheeks. They can hardly pull their high boots up over their pudgy toes."

She imagines him writing in the letter just for the fun of it: "This little piggy went to market. This little piggy stayed home. This little piggy had roast beef. This little piggy had none. This little piggy cried, 'Wee wee wee,' all the way home."

The next thing, Egon finds himself in a labor camp somewhere on the other side of the border. He is stuck in northern Germany. "*Ich bin wo?*" her startled father asks in *gebrochen* German.

Her mother tells her that her father dreams that he swallows huge slivers of glass during his nightmares. The glass shreds his throat while he dreams of cleaning up the streets after the blitz. He sees bloated bodies in the green air that swallows the streets in his dreams. He sees bodies floating in the canals of his dreams. That is why her dad's eyes turn green like the eye of the Dragon, Pia imagines.

One day, after about two years of camp, Egon is put on a train in the dark. Someone pushes him out of the door into the night. It's all over, he thinks to himself while he hangs suspended somewhere between the train and the earth below. Feeling the air sucked out behind him, he lands face down in a ditch. His mouth fills with mud.

"Where in the world am I? What just happened?" Egon wonders aloud as he walks across the fields spitting dirt. In the distance he sees a yellow light that pulls him like a magnet. He comes to a farm. He looks in through the window and sees a picture of King Christian X beside a row of blue-and-white porcelain Christmas tiles. The picture hangs a little askew on the wall above the farmer who snores loudly on the couch next to the fire. Egon is back in Denmark.

I'm in luck, he thinks to himself as he knocks on the green farmhouse door. Two years out of his life have passed. He is back, but he has a few nasty scars on his skinny white legs to prove his long stay away from home. Egon never shows his legs in public. "Never in public," he says.

Egon marries her mother after the war. Pia is born shortly after that event. In fact, she is born three months after they are married. Around eleven years of age, Pia snoops around her parents' papers in the left drawer of the cabinet that stands against the far wall in the living room.

Poking around for secrets, she finds that her father has been married twice before he married her mother. She has been told that her father had been married only once before in his life to a slut who is the mother of her half brother, Ralph. Or is it Alf? It is Ralph. She is sure it is Ralph.

She almost meets Ralph once when she sees her father throwing him out of the house. "Get out of my house," she hears her father yell across the table. Egon never wants to see Ralph's face again. Pia hears them talk about money. She remembers Ralph, a young man when her father throws him out of the house.

Pia finds her parents' marriage license in the left drawer of the cabinet in the living room. She reads it to herself. She is good at math, and she is good at reading. She is also good at teasing.

Of course, she has to tell her father the facts of his own life. He smacks her across the face. She deserves it. She deserves to be smacked. She likes to tease him. She likes to say: "You and Mommy did it before you married. You and Mommy did it. You did it."

Her mother marries her father in spite of the scars that mar his legs. Pia believes her mother thinks she is getting old and that her hopes for marriage are fast shrinking. She thinks her mother sees no other suitors around the corner. Her parents are both around thirty-six when they finally marry. "We better get married," Putte must have said to Egon. "You're the father of the baby in my belly."

Pia is a quiet baby. She doesn't walk until after her first birthday. She just lies on her back, staring into the sky above with her blue eyes. "You were such a good baby," her mother always tells her. Those are her mother's words. Her whole life, her mother tells her that she was a good baby.

Her parents tell her that they can't decide what name to give her. "Should we call her Lisbeth?" they argue. "Should we name her Pia?" In the end, they settle on Pia. She imagines, when later told of their debate, that her parents threw the rejected Lisbeth out in the street as her father had done her half brother, Ralph. Like the Little Match Girl, Lisbeth is now the one who looks in through the window. Pia is sure that Lisbeth is the one who wants her Christmas tree. She is the one who wants her goose for dinner.

Her parents name her brother Poul after the suicidal cousin. The brother is born two and a half years after Pia. He is a beautiful baby, too. Her parents are in luck. "We are in luck," they say. They have two beautiful children. "...A girl for you. A boy for me. Oh," they sing in harmony, "can't you see how happy we will be."

CHAPTER 8

My pace is not my normal pace this morning. I'm afraid that my story will fade away before I can capture the words. I have always been high-strung and nervous, and I'm aware that I'm inclined to hysteria, but I feel even more tense than usual when I wake up at 5:17.

I can't sleep any longer. I am not my real self this early morning. I usually sleep till eight or nine in my white king-size bed. As a rule, I watch TV, switching back and forth between CNN and Channel 4. I watch Katie Couric smile at me before I get up for my morning cup of coffee while I read the *Los Angeles Times* at a pace that suits me.

Caron inherits my bad traits. She is a screamer. I used to be a screamer, too. Now, I'm a reformed screamer. When Caron enters the room, I feel as if I am walking on eggshells. My arms get tight around my chest. For a small person, Caron takes up a lot of space.

Suzanna, on the other hand, is calm. She is as calm as a still lake after a storm. Suzanna can't take any stress. She avoids stress at all cost. She puts her head under the pillow until the stress goes away.

Yesterday, at El Coyote Restaurant on Beverly Boulevard, we sit, Suzanna and I, on the patio. Across from me at the red table under the red plastic awning that covers our heads, Suzanna tells me that she thinks it's only fitting that Caron should end up with two babies at the same time. I take a sip of my margarita on the rocks with salt and look at her over the rim of my glass. I'm quiet. "It's her fate," Suzanna goes on. "It's her lot in life."

"It's her lot in life," she repeats, stressing the word "lot." She continues in a tone of self-assuredness, stating that she believes that Caron is too possessive of her and that Caron will try to control the twins as she has done her. "They will unite against their mother as they grow up. They'll gang up against Caron," she announces with conviction.

I guess she is right. Suzanna is usually right. She is straight as an arrow, and she is single-minded. "There is power in numbers," Suzanna says, stressing the word "power." "Caron will be too distracted with two of them to be able to rein them in."

"The two of them will climb the walls," she continues in her righteous voice, without missing a beat. "They'll drop out of the windows. They'll fall down the stairs. They'll crack their heads open. They'll break their front teeth. They'll break their fingers."

"They're her lot in life," Suzanna says, stressing the word "lot" once again. "They'll be a life lesson to her." That's how Suzanna thinks, always pragmatic. I'm not really listening any longer. I'm getting lost in my own thoughts drinking my margarita across from her. I lick the salt off the glass. Did Suzanna say that they would break their fingers?

I look down at the scar on the tip of my slightly crooked left middle finger, and I'm reminded of my first encounter with a set of twins. I remember visiting two little girls with my mother in a large apartment across from the Lakes in Copen-hagen. My mother and their mother, busy drinking coffee and eating cookies, sat in the living room while the three of us were running around in all the other rooms playing a game of tag.

The pair of twins, Anne and Mette, had pulled the door shut while the mothers sat on the couch. The door had jammed on Pia's finger. I see myself at the age of two, looking up at the doctor. Pia looked up at him with the little smile of hers after he had just sewn back the tip of her middle left finger. Her little smile kept back the tears. "Here," the doctor said, handing her an orange. "You are such a good girl. You don't even cry."

I see myself smiling at my first taste of an orange just when I hear Suzanna raise her voice across from me, "You never listen, Mom. You're always so distracted." Suzanna invariably grumbles when she sees me disappearing into my own thoughts.

"I'm listening. I heard you. And what do you mean by distracted? I've got my feet on the ground. I heard you say that Caron is too controlling," I nod my head in agreement. Naturally, I ask Suzanna if she thinks I'm too controlling also.

"Controlling?" I can see that Suzanna keeps her thoughts to herself. "No, you're just protective, which is a good thing in a mother." She makes a reassuring smile.

Of course, I shouldn't have asked Caron about the future names of my grandchildren. She definitely considers that sort of question a meddling question. I could hear it in her voice. "You're meddling," it said. Even over the phone that hangs in the kitchen, her voice got that irritated tone.

My intentions were good. I just wanted to protect the names of my grandchildren. I only needed to remind Caron once more that she shouldn't give them dog names like Wolfie and Rolfie. But if truth be told, I also wanted to protect myself from any more embarrassment than it is necessary to encounter in this life.

Caron changed her family name to Skovmand a few years

earlier. Skovmand is my maiden name. In Danish it means a common woodsman, not even a forester. Not particularly elegant or blueblood sounding. Not elegant at all. She changed her name because she preferred the sound of Caron Skovmand.

Caron felt that the name of Skovmand was dying out. She felt it was her duty to maintain the family line. "Your duty is it? I beg your pardon," I responded in my sarcastic voice. "Your duty?" I thought it disrespectful to throw away her father's name. "Is he a pair of dirty old socks?" I asked her.

"Please, don't change your name," I begged her. "The name of Skovmand is a curse." I paused for a second to regain my composure. "A curse," I repeated, not wanting to lose my temper completely. "My father is a loser. His entire family is a bunch of losers. My grandmother, who married a Skovmand, is a loser. She was a coldhearted woman. She didn't have a heart. Her heart was cold."

I heard the stories of my grandmother's cold heart for years after she had died. I heard that she chased my grandfather around the table with a large butcher knife raised high in her hand. The knife almost stabbed him. She had her own reasons to stab him, of course. I'm sure she had her reasons. But, for God's sake, we all have to learn to control our tempers. It is a curse to lose your temper.

I remember that while growing up in Valby, Pia could see for herself that her grandmother's eyes no longer looked fiery behind the wire-framed glasses she wore in the photograph that stood in the fake silver frame on top of the cabinet against the far wall of the living room. Pia saw then in the black-and-white photograph that her grandmother's eyes, the color of steel just like her father's, had let go of her bad temper long ago. They showed not a hint of anger.

In that same photograph, three-year-old Pia stands next to the perfect grandmother whose white hair sits piled high in a bun on top of her head. The child is dressed in a pretty gingham dress with a small white collar tight around her neck. Pia, looking at the photograph, remembers the dress being made of a light-blue cotton. The child, with a hand on her grandmother's arm, has a little mindful smile on her face. Her baby brother, displayed in a long white christening gown in the grandmother's arms, looks like a girl.

Pia sees the only picture of the three of them together on the cabinet. It reminds her of the only memory she has of her grandmother alive. The memory begins with the fairy tale of "Little Red Riding Hood." She remembers the sinking feeling of doom in her stomach when she is three.

Her mother reads her the story while she follows along looking at the color pictures in the book. Pia sees Little Red Riding Hood's grandmother looking just like her own grandmother. They both have wrinkles and white hair. They both wear little round glasses low upon their noses. In the pictures, the grandmother's plum-colored bedspread looks the same color as her grandmother's. White chamber pots stand under both their beds.

When her mother comes to the part where the Big Bad Wolf eats the grandmother and crawls in under the plum-colored bedspread, Pia grows wild with rage. She can't believe that the grandmother says something this foolish over and over again: "Oh my, what big eyes you have. What big...! What big...!"

Pia throws herself down, beating the floorboards with

her small fists and her head. "My grandmother is dead," she screams. "She is dead. My grandmother is dead in the stomach of the Big Bad Wolf." Furiously crying because she sees the horror of her grandmother being dead in the wolf's stomach, Pia is still able to think to herself that her grandmother would have had time to get out of bed if she hadn't been so busy talking to the wolf.

Pia is certain that her real grandmother is now churning around in the stomach of the Big Bad Wolf. Her mother, unable to console her, stops reading her the story before the wolf eats Little Red Riding Hood. It is only years later that Pia learns that the wolf also eats Little Red Riding Hood after he eats the grandmother.

I'll read the story of "Little Red Riding Hood" to the twins soon. I want to see their eyes turn big when it becomes clear to them that the Big Bad Wolf has swallowed their beloved grandmother. I want to see the sad tears roll down their cheeks when they realize that their grandmother is turning to mush in the stomach of the horrible wolf. They'll miss her deeply. They will miss her.

"We can't live without her," they'll scream while they bang their heads against the floorboards. "Where's Granny?" they'll scream. I want them to remember their granny always even if they think she is a little foolish.

I will tell the twins this when I read them the story of "Little Red Riding Hood": "If you live long enough, you may have the good fortune of becoming grandparents, too. You may in the end grow as foolish as I am. The pleasure of living long enough is knowing that bad things happen to all of us. Just ask the granny who churns in the stomach of the Big Bad Wolf. She knows it better than anyone."

"I'm listening. I heard you," I repeat to Suzanna, who by now looks irritated across from me. I take another sip of my margarita and go on, "It's better to be foolish than controlling, is it not?" Soon to be a granny, I decide not to reveal how amusing I find it to be thinking of the Big Bad Wolf eating Granny for dinner at a restaurant named El Coyote. Suzanna shakes her head, not bothering to answer me.

CHAPTER 9

Boom. 1 2 3, boom. 4 5 6, boom. 7 8 9, boom. 10, boom. Denmark Norway Sweden, boom. Finland Iceland Greenland, boom. Germany France England, boom. Italy, boom. Red white blue, boom. Green yellow brown, boom. Purple orange pink, boom. Black, boom. The pink ball hits the yellow brick wall. Boom. The blue ball hits the wall. Boom. One pink. One blue.

Pia likes to keep track when she is ten. She likes to measure her life in Valby from top to bottom. She tries to list each and every thing she knows in the universe. She doesn't let up for hours, repeating her list of subjects: colors, countries, cities, animals, boy names, girl names, street names, numbers, on and on they are ticked off one by one.

There is no stopping her. She has a system of throwing the balls and saying the words out loud when the ball hits against the yellow brick wall. She must always say the names in the exact order each time, and the ball must never fall. She always ends with a "boom" after three hits.

No stopping the balls. Boom. Boom. She is on a roll. Boom. Don't drop the ball. One blue. One pink. Don't drop the ball. Keep them moving. Throw with the right hand. Catch with the left. A B C, boom. D E F, boom. One blue. One pink. Boom. Tiger lion elephant, boom. Dog, cat...

"...Pia!" She turns around. She sees old Mrs. Madsen dressed in her Sunday best. Pia's eyes turn black when she hears Mrs. Madsen call her name on the street. Just as the bird's eyes turn hard when it sees its tiny egg roll out of the nest into the green bushes, Pia's eyes turn icy and sharp when she sees her ball roll away down the street.

The pink ball bounces merrily into the bushes. She is going to kill Mrs. Madsen now. She is going to aim her ball right at the crack between Mrs. Madsen's two breasts. She wants to see Mrs. Madsen fall over in her green dress with the flowers strewn across it. She wants to see Mrs. Madsen's large breasts droop down to the grass like two old wrinkled apples fallen from the tree among the red and yellow flowers on her dress.

Pia imagines that she throws her blue ball right at the dark crack between the two breasts. She imagines Mrs. Madsen falling down dead upon her broad back squarely on the street. People will say, "Poor thing. Pia's blue ball did it. Mrs. Madsen died not knowing what hit her. Things happen. She couldn't take the shock. It was an accident. Mrs. Madsen's luck ran out."

Instead, Mrs. Madsen hands her a couple of crowns for some goods and a quarter for her trouble. She asks her in a sweet voice, "Pia, please run down to the baker. Would you please get me some rolls and a bottle of milk, honey?"

Pia looks down at the quarter in her hand. Mrs. Madsen calls her "honey." She loves Mrs. Madsen. She is the best person in the world. She wants to kiss the rouge on Mrs. Madsen's cheek. She wants to hug the round bosom in Mrs. Madsen's green dress with the red and yellow flowers. A whole quarter.

She flies down the street, past number 23, number 21, number 19, down the stone stairs at the end of the block, past the hardware store, around the corner. She flies into the bakery. At least three people stand in line ahead of her. She looks at the jars of licorice on the counter. What to buy, she ponders. Two large round ones? Five round smaller ones? She decides: two small round ones and a bunch of the little diamond-shaped ones.

She loves Mrs. Madsen best of all in the whole world. Eight licorice diamonds make a perfect star in the middle of the top of her hand. She loves Mrs. Madsen to death. She licks the star. She licks. Lick. Lick. Lick.

Her tongue turns black. The diamonds melt into one large black hole in the universe of her hand. She licks. Oh, the taste of sweet salt. "Oh, Mrs. Madsen, here are your rolls," Pia says with a little guilty smile when she returns from the store. "Here is your milk." She is relieved that she doesn't have to say to the sweet Mrs. Madsen, "I'm sorry. I didn't really mean to kill you in your Sunday best."

It's eight in the morning by now. It's time for breakfast. It is Sunday. Sunday is the best day. The house smells of her father's freshly baked rolls. Her dumb little brother sits next to her father across from her. The three of them sit at the table. Poul's Dumbo ears reach for the shores of Sweden, and his auburn hair stands straight up like a thousand quills on a warped porcupine.

Poul's hazel eyes are filled with whitish green pus and sleep. One is blind. Egon and Pia can't tell it is blind. The family doesn't even know his one eye is blind until they get a note from the school nurse: "We regret to inform you that your son, Poul Skovmand, is blind in his left eye."

"It's blind?" they ask, looking around at one another. We look at his left eye. We look at his right eye. The two look the same. No difference, they think. Life is not fair. Poul is not lucky in life. What can you do about your fate in life?

They sit at the breakfast table, the three of them. Her father wears his white tank top undershirt. His trucker's arms, red to the elbows, rest on the table. The remainder of him is the color of pure white bacon lard. She sees the ashen gray color of his face. A dark blue pigment fills the half-moon circles under his eyes. What's left of his dark hair is combed through with greasy brilliantine. Two bald spots curve back from both sides of his forehead, and the few hairs loitering on top cover the middle like a shredded rug.

Poul and Pia drink hot coffee with lots of warm milk. Egon drinks it black with a ton of sugar. They silently eat the hot rolls speckled with silvery poppy seeds on the golden crust. They spread thick layers of creamy butter on the rolls. They spread the butter. Butter. Butter. Butter. They don't speak a word. They are in heaven.

They hear Perry sing in his cage. Perry always sings in his cage except when it's dark. Pia names the blue parakeet Perry after Perry Como. She loves Perry Como. She loves it when Perry sings, "One of these mornin's you're gonna rise up singin'. Then you'll spread your wings, and you'll take to the sky." She wants Perry Como to be her daddy. She thinks that Perry looks sweet and gentle. Perry wears cardigan sweaters, and he has lots of beautiful hair.

Her daddy, his head big and gray on his high shoulders, smokes the last cigarette he has on him. His huge right hand crumples the package, and he hands Pia a couple of crowns. "Run down to the corner," he commands. "Get me another package of cigarettes. Get me a pack."

She flies up from the chair. She'll do anything for her daddy. She flies down the stairs, past number 23, number 21, number

19, down the stone stairs at the end of the block, past the hardware store, around the corner, past the bakery.

The tall skinny machine leans against the wall next to the entrance to the bar. She puts two crowns into the slot. She pulls at the second to the left knob. Down drops the package of ten filterless Cecils. Cecil is written across the white front in cursive green letters. She thinks the letters look pretty. What a pretty name. Just like Cecilia, she thinks.

She flies back to number 25. She flies up the stairs covered in dirty brown linoleum. She flies past the oily yellow walls in the hallway. She opens the door to the left, and she flies into the living room.

She sees the green couch, which doubles as her bed, against the wall away from the corner windows where the yellow curtains hang. She sees the cabinet with the three doors topped by three drawers against the far wall. Each and every thing in the world is behind the three doors: the dishes, the papers, the books, the pencils, the linens.

She sees another, smaller cabinet to her left. Slide the doors to the sides, and her brother's bed is in there behind the doors. Every night it is folded out, taking up most of the space left in the living room. Her brother sleeps in the pullout bed with his crystal radio set attached to his ears, listening for sounds that travel through the air.

Pia flies in through the door. She sees the black square coal stove in the corner. It is the same stove her mother and Poul and she had huddled around when they moved to Valby from number 8B in Christianshavn about two years earlier. The new home felt too grand to keep warm in then. They didn't yet feel warm and cozy in number 25.

Her father converts the coal stove into an oil stove. Once a week or so, they pour oil into the container stored on the other side of the wall in the little red entrance hall. The oil flows slowly into the stove as it is needed. Sometimes the house smells of oil. "It is easier to live with the smell of oil than dragging home a bucket of coal every day," her father tells them. They all nod their heads in agreement.

Pia flies in. She sees her father in his green wing chair. He sits in the only soft chair in the room. She sees the clock that hangs on the wall above her brother's cabinet bed to the left. It strikes: boing, boing, boing, boing, boing, boing, boing, boing, boing, boing. It's ten in the morning.

Her father sits from early in the morning waiting for the clock to strike eight, when the evening news begins. She hands him the pack of Cecils. She kisses him on his gray cheek. She loves her daddy more than anything in the world. He is the best daddy. Her brother vanishes for the day. He is off.

She tiptoes out the door. Her father is asleep in the green chair that he dies in alone twenty-three years later. He sleeps in the same chair that he would be sitting in dead for three days with the television still running before someone finds him.

Pia tiptoes out the door down to the street. Other kids are outside playing by now. She joins them. They play ball. They jump rope. They play hopscotch. Pia's glass stone is perfect. It's shaped like a small round pancake that shines bright purple in the light. The bottom used to be a shiny purple before it turned a grayish color during the scraping and the sliding against the cement.

The bottom of the stone also used to curve up a bit. Now, it is perfectly gray and smooth. That's how a stone should look:

flat at the bottom. She kicks the stone gently. Just so, it moves buttery soft across the white chalk line. She sees it stop at the exact upper corner of the square.

She kicks the stone gently again. It lands in the middle of the square in a soft swoop. She loves her purple stone as much as she did her red one that broke in half when it once hit the yellow brick wall. Now the purple stone is as good as her red, Pia thinks to herself as the Sundays of her young life slide across the white chalk line into the corner of the next square.

CHAPTER 10

Boom. 1 2 3, boom. 4 5 6, boom. 7 8 9, boom. 10, boom. Denmark Norway Sweden, boom. Finland Iceland Greenland, boom. Germany France England, boom. Italy, boom. Red white blue, boom.

It's another cold Sunday on the street. Pia needs her jacket to keep warm. She drags her feet up the dirty brown stairs to the first floor. Afraid that she'll wake her daddy, she stands hesitating a moment to pull out the key and turn it in the lock.

She looks to her right where Kristine lives behind the door with her beautiful mom and handsome dad. They are quiet and polite behind the door to the right. Kristine's father doesn't drink and her mother never wears a hat, except when it is cold outside. Kristine is an only child. Kristine is beautiful. Kristine is lucky.

Pia takes the key that dangles on the string off her neck and turns it softly in the door. She tiptoes in. She hears her father snoring in his green chair. Her father works six days a week from morning to night, and on Sundays he sleeps in his green chair.

She tiptoes past the chair and opens the door slowly into her parents' bedroom. "Please, don't squeak," she prays. She wants her blue jacket that hangs in the closet behind the mirror. She sees the crack in the mirror that her father once caused after he woke up from one of his nightmares. He broke the mirror by hitting at his own reflection after he swallowed huge pieces of glass in his dreams.

Pia stood in the doorway after he cracked the mirror. She saw her father alone on the edge of the bed. She watched from behind, her father's head bent low, resting in his hands. The elbows stuck into his knees. She looked across the bed into the mirror and saw the crack opening wide through the top of his head.

She saw the crack becoming a crevice. She saw Doubting Thomas and Prince Hamlet dangling off the edge. She heard the two of them beg the answer across the great divide in her father's head to the one and only lasting question echoing off the walls of the abyss: "To be, or not to be?" Barely hanging on by their fingernails, Thomas and Hamlet clung to the steep cliff in dread of the answer soon to come.

Or did she break it? Her brother had torn up her books that line the two shelves in the little bookcase in her parents' bedroom. She threw an ink bottle at her brother's Dumbo ears. He ducked, and the bottle hit the mirror. She saw her reflection in the mirror with the crack right down the middle. She stood bursting with rage, ready to kill her brother.

She broke the mirror, knowing that if the mirror breaks, bad luck sits like the guest of honor at the table for years until he begins to smell like rotten fish, and nothing gets him out the door. The guest sits festering in his chair until the last hour of the seventh year.

Pia looks at herself in the cracked mirror. She pulls the jacket over her head and tightens the hood around her face to keep out the wind that blows on the street. The jacket is made of heavy blue cotton. She sees the large pocket in front. It is a perfect size. It is large enough to hold her rubber balls and her purple stone.

"Pia," her father yells. "What in the hell are you doing? Why are you making so much noise? Why?" The paw slaps her across the face. The Big Bad Wolf has just been woken out of his sleep. She sees the shadow of the wolf hovering over her. Smack. The wolf leaves a red mark across her face. The red mark never goes away.

When the twins grow up and people ask them why their grandmother has that funny red mark across her face, they'll answer, "It's nothing. The wolf swallowed her when she went to visit her grandmother in the forest. The wolf was ashamed of himself. He coughed her up. She was embarrassed to tell, so her cheek turned red. It's just a little red. It's nothing."

The wolf strikes her again across the ear. Smack. The ear turns bright red. When people ask the twins why their grandmother's ear is so red, they'll answer, "The wolf ate her. He was ashamed of himself. He coughed her up. She was embarrassed to tell, so her ear turned red. It's nothing." They will laugh. "It's only a little red," they will say.

The wolf howls, "Go to bed. Leave me alone. Leave me in peace. Can't you ever be quiet? Be quiet."

"Go to bed." Pia creeps into bed in her parents' bedroom. She is scared. She wants to die. She hates her daddy. She tears the sheets on the bed to shreds. Fire spews from her nose. She gags. She cries into the pillow, "I'll kill him. He will die. He will go to hell. It's his bad luck. He is out of luck."

The wolf is back in his green chair. He sits half asleep again, knowing that he sends her to bed for good reasons of his own: one, so that he can sleep undisturbed in his chair, and two, so that he won't have to worry about her running loose on the street. It's the best solution he can come up with on Sundays when he is resting, bone tired from the week's work.

Pia waits in bed for her mother to come home. Her mother

always works at the hotel on Sundays. Then she takes the train home four stops to Hvidovre Station from central Copenhagen. The train arrives at 3:27 in the afternoon. The train is always on time.

Her mother walks through the tunnel, past the empty field on her left, through the park, up the stairs, down the block, past number 19, number 21, number 23, to number 25. She walks up the stairs in heavy and slow steps wearing her green hat.

"Never go out in public without a hat," her mother says in her green hat.

"It's ugly, that hat," Pia tells her mother.

Why can't she look smart and young like Kristine's mom? Why does she have to be short and fat and old and ugly? Why does she wear a green hat?

Her mother walks into the living room. "Hello, Egon," she greets him sweetly. He sits in his green coffin. Only he doesn't know it, the bastard. He is out of luck, the bastard.

"What's the matter, Egon?" Pia hears her mother ask in a meek voice that travels through the bedroom door. "Oh, Egon. Let her get up," she hears her mother plead with her father. "She will be good. Come, Pia, kiss your daddy. Kiss your daddy and make up."

Pia gets out of bed. She sees her mother's hazel eyes, tired behind the glasses, pleading with her. She doesn't want to kiss her daddy. She doesn't want to make up. She wants to spit in her mother's eye. She wants to kick her black-and-blue. She wants to kick her like the dog she is. Kick the dog, she thinks. She wants to break her mother's bones into a pile of splinters.

Pia kisses her daddy. She smells the smoke on his gray stubbly cheek when it scratches her lips. She puts on her blue anorak jacket. She flies out the door. Dinner at six. Two more hours.

She is on the swing. She swings. She swings away to her father in Hollywood where he sings to her: "...there's a nothin' can harm you, with Daddy and Mammy standin' by...."

In Hollywood, Pia and Perry sit next to Fred Astaire and Ginger Rogers at the long Formica counter. They order their own sweet rolls at the counter in Hollywood, Perry and she. They drink strawberry ice cream sodas through long pink straws. The cherry on the whipped cream reaches high above their heads. Perry takes her hand and they skip down the boulevard. They skip into the zoo. People look at her. They say, "There goes Perry's daughter. Isn't she pretty? Isn't she lucky?"

"Isn't she lucky?" people ask one another on the streets of Hollywood. They say that she is lucky. They say that you make your own luck in Hollywood. Pia knows that only lucky people say things like that. She knows that luck finds you or it doesn't find you. Luck is luck. The rest is balderdash.

Don't be crybabies. Don't be wimps. Don't be bores. Don't whine that my mother did this, Pia says to herself as she swings back and forth on her swing. Don't whine that your father did that. Balderdash. Balderdash. Balderdash. She loves that word: *balderdash*.

Caron has her own room. Caron has her own bed on Kagel Canyon in the town of Arleta. She has no sister until she is twelve. She goes to the ponies on Sundays with her dad. She goes to the Big Boy Restaurant with her mother in Century City. She eats a sandwich with the bacon crossed just so on the orange cheddar cheese. She drinks a glass of cold milk. We talk and laugh.

We laugh again. We shop for clothes. We go to the park. I

push her on the swing. I keep on pushing her. Back and forth, she swings. We skip across the park. We skip home. She takes a bubble bath in the white bathtub. I kiss her on her wet stomach. I read her the story about the bear eating stone soup.

I tuck her into bed. I rub her legs. What's what? My mother and my father, they took care of me. They gave me a roof over my head. They fed me. They kept me warm. They kissed me. They loved me. They adored me. They gave me more than enough. Why can't Caron ever get enough? Why can't she ever be happy? Caron is a bore. Caron is a wimp. I never wear a green hat. I feel sorry for the twins that Caron is going to be their mother. I'm glad she is not my mother.

It is six in the evening. Pia has left her swing for the dinner that waits on the table at home. She sits down with the family. They eat fried sausages and stewed green kale and peeled new potatoes. They eat prunes and apricot compote with thick yellow cream for dessert. She loves her mommy. She loves her daddy.

Her daddy sits in his green chair. Her mommy darns her father's black sock at the table after the dishes have been cleared. Her mother sits on the dining room chair covered in stained yellow damask. The yellow light shines above her head. Her hazel eyes close behind her glasses.

The father and the brother and she listen to the radio. "The Russians are coming. The Russians are coming," the voice repeats on the news. They hear it over and over again. The Russians are always coming. She knows to watch out for the Russians and the Yellow Hordes. She never laughs and makes fun of the news.

"Putte, wake up. Wake up, Putte," says Egon. Putte's head

hits the table with a heavy thonk. *Putte* means little and cute and adorable. Putte is a saint.

Her mother gets up at five in the morning to feed Egon his breakfast of hot coffee and toast with butter and strawberry jam. Egon goes off to work at six in the morning. Putte goes to the hotel at seven. Work. Work. Work. Six days a week, they work. They work from morning to night. Only Sunday, Egon is home all day. Pia loves Sundays. "Putte, wake up," her daddy says to her mommy again in Valby.

Boom. 1 2 3, boom. 4 5 6, boom. 7 8 9, boom. 10, boom. Denmark Norway Sweden, boom. It's another Sunday.

CHAPTER 11

I see the ghosts hovering around the table. They always come back at Christmastime. "Hey, we know you. We know you," they say. "Hey, I know you too," I say, pricking them with my fork.

Caron, now about eight months old, is sleeping in her crib in the bedroom, and I am sitting at the blue kitchen table next to the window in Stockholm. "And I know you and you and you," I tell the ghosts once again. "What happened to you? Where did you go? Come, let me feed you. Let me hug you and kiss you. Let me smell you. Come, let's have supper."

"Tread softly," the voices whisper across the table. "Be ever mindful. Be reverent. Soar light. Be strong. Be kind. Be firm," they whisper. "Look valiant. Act generous. Be fearless," they whisper. "Be thoughtful. Be stoic. Be straight. Stand tall. Be silent."

I hear the voices floating toward me across the table. I see the space that divides me from them who whisper from the other side. I see the fine line in the sand. I see the still point where rage touches love. I see the border where desire faces repulsion. I want to reach across the line and touch them. I want to kiss them. I want to turn away. Why are you bothering me? Go away, all of you.

I look out upon the snow. A white blanket covers the roofs of the cars, and the branches of the trees hang low with the heaviness of ice in their veins. It is silent now between me and them across the table. I cannot hear the whisper any longer. It is silent.

Here it is in a nutshell, I think to myself. I'll put my head on the pillow of snow. I will dream of fire. I will dream of food in my stomach. I will cross the line. We will touch again at the still point.

I look out the window at the snow piling high. I see the Volkswagen bus standing like a large snowdrift next to the smaller snowdrifts in the parking lot. We have bought the bus just recently from an English friend when passing through London on our way to Denmark from Seattle. The bus is old, with those two small side windows in front that you can push in and out. It has right-hand drive. It has no heat, and it is yellow under the snow.

After visiting my parents in Valby for a few weeks, we drive the bus from Copenhagen to Stockholm at a speed of about fifty miles an hour. We drive it through carved-out icebergs. Fenced in between the snow plowed high on each side of the road, I cannot hear a sound.

It is silent here in Sweden, I think. Oh, so silent. I look behind me, seeing only whiteness through the rear window. I notice Caron in her crib bed in the back of the car. I see through the mesh that her face has turned purple from the cold.

"Stop the car," I demand. "We must bring her up here so I can keep her warm." I look at Jeffrey with an anger that is greater than the silence between us. I choke on anger. I spew fire.

He stops the car with the same sudden jerk he had made when he stopped our lives abruptly in Seattle after quitting his good job as a news reporter on television. He had been the golden boy brought up from film school at UCLA. He flashed on the screen every night speaking his opinions, and people listened. Jeffrey has more opinions than there are dead soldiers in Vietnam, I used to think to myself.

But no. He had to leave. We packed up the house we had bought on Queen Anne Hill. We pulled up our stakes after living in Seattle for nearly two years. Caron was about three months old when Jeffrey decided that we were going to Sweden on a dream and a penny in our pocket. He believed he had a job waiting for him at the Swedish Film School. We were off. Goodbye house. Goodbye friends. Goodbye family. Goodbye Nixon. Goodbye America. Goodbye.

Now, Jeffrey trusts that he is going to teach film to a bunch of dreary Swedes groveling in the footsteps of Ingmar Bergman. Bergman? Bah humbug. Films filled with old clocks: tick tock, tick tock. Wild strawberries up my ass. Chessboards and skeletons. Silence and doves. Silence in my ear.

We breathe the air of silence in Sweden. We eat silence for dinner. It makes you puke. I hate it. I hate Bergman. I hate Jeffrey. I hate myself. I hate the snow. I hate the blue. Everything, except the snow, is blue here: the walls, the tiles, the tables, the rya rugs. Icy blue like my heart.

The baby is asleep in the bedroom. I walk into the bathroom, which is covered in shiny blue tiles. I clean the mirror. I wipe and wipe. I wipe some more. The blue shines bluer than ever.

It won't go away, I think to myself.

"I'm better off dead," I say out loud, speaking to the silence. "Jeffrey is better off with me dead. Caron is better off. The world is better off."

The blueness drowns me. I sink down on my knees and place my head against the tiled floor. It feels cool against my forehead. I pray for black as I speak to the silence. "Please, dear God. Forgive me for feeling so blue. Please, let me die. I'm worthless as it is."

I tell the silence, "I'm so sorry that I can't make it." I see the razor blade through the corner of my eye. It lies at a sharp angle on the upper corner of the blue tile. With my forehead pressed against the cool floor, I wonder how it feels to make a swift cut. How would the blade feel against my skin?

My third eye sees the deep-red blood flowing across the floor and slithering over the tiles into the blue grout. It moves slowly into curvy shapes just as the red gel does when it heats up in the lava lamp on the blue corner table. It flows out the door and down the steps. It seeps into the pure white snow. Red cherry juice spreads through crushed ice in the cone.

The eye sees the floor lifting itself up off the ground. It transforms into a blue wavy carpet floating up into the air with me on top bent over on my knees. The eye sees the carpet move slowly upward and out through the door as it unravels into a string of bluebirds flailing their wings behind me across the pink crushed ice. I think, kneeling with my forehead on the carpet, that the birds look sad and drab dangling on the string. Why are they so sad?

I don't die. My third eye and the bluebirds are lone and curious witnesses to my ascent. I don't cut my wrist. I don't put my head in the oven. I don't lay my head on the ice and close my eyes as did Oetzi the Iceman, whose frozen mummy was found in the Alps five thousand years later.

I don't lay my head on the ice and look across the mountains. My eye doesn't catch the whiteness as far as it can see. I don't lay my head on the ice and dream of red deer meat in my stomach.

I don't dream of thick creamy goat milk and chewy grains. I don't dream of the fire that flamed in Oetzi's last dream when he lowered his head on the ice and closed his eyes. Not yet.

The baby cries. I lift myself off the floor. The bluebirds of happiness flap away. They are small black dots flickering in front of my eyes. I empty out the trash can instead. I take the trash out into the hallway and drop it into the metal chute that opens in the wall. I hear the hollow sound of the trash falling.

I go back into Caron's room. She is standing up in her crib holding on to the railing. She tries to pull herself out. Her face and hair are wet from sleep and tears. I lift her out of the crib. I put my nose into her damp neck. It smells sweet like cotton candy. I carry her to the window, and we look out onto the thick layer of snow together. "Look," I say cheerfully. "See the pink cotton candy. Isn't it pretty?"

She presses her small hand against the cold glass as if she sees the cotton candy. I nuzzle my nose into the folds of her neck. I don't say to her, "The snow looks like Cy Twombly's *Rose of Sentimental Despair*." Why in the world would I say that? After all, before full-blown despair, it is on this day yet a faint brush stroke in the painter's eye. I would never say that. Would I?

I take Caron back into the living room and sit down on the blue couch next to the glass table that stands on the blue rya rug. I look down upon my left finger. Where is my ring? Where is the wedding ring that Jeffrey bought for me at the flea market in Paris twenty-five hundred or so days ago? Where is my ring inscribed with the words: "I love you more than yesterday, less than tomorrow"? Where is it?

I walk into the bathroom. It is not there. I know where it

is. I know it as sure as the world here is blue. It has gone down the chute with the trash. It has been sucked into the trash bin. It has punched a hole through the atmosphere, leaving a huge vacuum in its trail.

Oh, my God. It has all come to this, I think to myself. What is left of my heart has fallen into the trash of the universe. I try calling the building manager. I finally reach him at eight in the evening. I tell him in Danish, "You must come. You must open up the trash room in the basement right away."

"No way," he answers me in a drunken Swedish voice. "I'll come tomorrow. You'll have to wait. I'm not going anywhere tonight."

"But the garbage men are picking up tomorrow. You must let me in," I beg him.

"I'll be there tomorrow at eight," he answers in his snooty way before he hangs up on me. He tries to hide the fact that he is drunk. But he can't lie to me. I know that all he wants is a few more beers before he falls into bed.

Jeffrey sleeps beside me. He doesn't care. He sleeps away his worries. There is no job here. There never was a job waiting for him. He had been promised a position at the film school. But when we finally arrived in Stockholm, the job had been filled by a Swede. Now we and a bunch of draft dodgers, along with a few out-of-work Swedes, are on welfare here during the Vietnam War.

Thank heaven for Swedish welfare. We may be trapped in an apartment, paid for by the Swedish government, in a suburb south of Stockholm called Traangsund, but it is nice. Oh, so nice it is, here in Traangsund. We are comfortable and safe in our apartment while Jeffrey waits for another job to come through at Swedish Television. Now he sleeps beside me, and the snow keeps falling from the sky.

Eight the next morning, I meet the manager in front of the room of garbage in the basement. He is grouchy and unfriendly. I smell the beer behind the coffee breath. He stoops, looking bored and rumpled, as he opens the steel door with his key. The stench of human lives greets us. It floats out from the gray cement walls. I see twelve feet by twelve feet of holy space filled with the week's garbage.

I look across the field of cans and paper and rotten apples and orange peel and chicken bones. I see a piece of white paper, a soft and innocent cloud floating above the peaks and valleys of human waste. I stretch my arm across the stench. I raise the cloud gingerly between my right forefinger and thumb.

There it is. There is my little gold ring resting in a sweet and tender circle on top of the world's garbage. I see the glow of rose gold revealed under a piece of toilet paper. I reach out for the gold ring. I pick it up gently and slip it back on my finger. It's a little too big. I kiss it. I see all the tomorrows ahead of me. No, I will not die yet.

Here it is in a nutshell, I think to myself. I'll not put my head on the pillow of snow. I will not yet dream of fire. I will not yet cross the line. The ghosts and I will not yet touch hands at the still point. No, I will not die yet.

CHAPTER 12

I do not die. I do not cut my wrist on the bathroom floor in the suburb of Stockholm. Rather, I scrape the snow off the roof of the yellow Volkswagen bus parked in front of our kitchen window. The snowflakes flutter in a dance, making a soft landing on the white snowdrifts piled high on the side of the road.

Jeffrey and I drive the newly swept car to the welfare office, where we have to get some official papers in order. It is almost Christmas Eve. The Swedes are hidden behind their doors. We see the candles lit in the windows. They are so cozy behind their windows. We are the only clients at the welfare office this late in the evening.

We decide to stop for dinner on the way home. We find a little cafeteria open in a corner building that looks just like all the other yellow brick buildings in the neighborhood. Except for one man sitting alone at a blue table, we are the only other diners in the place.

All they serve is spaghetti. There is no Christmas goose and rice pudding here. We fill our plates. We put Caron in the high chair. It's dark under the low lights. There are no candles on the tables in this cafeteria. We don't speak much.

The lone diner wakes up over his plate of spaghetti. He looks up and pushes back his chair. He weaves between the empty tables over to our blue table. He smells drunk as a skunk. "The Swedes are cold as ice, aren't they?" he asks us in broken English after he finally reaches our table. "You are Americans, aren't you?"

"Yeah," Jeffrey answers reluctantly.

"I myself, I am Norwegian," the man informs us in a slurred voice. "May I join you?"

He sits down without waiting for an answer, muttering something unintelligible. We all eat on in silence. After about five minutes, the Norwegian wakes up again. This time he grabs Jeffrey's hand. He turns the hand over and looks at the palm close up.

"You have the Star of David in your hand," he mumbles in his sloshed tone. "Your life will change when you turn thirty-seven. You will find success then."

I look at the man in horror. Jeffrey is thirty-two. Five more years. They seem an eternity.

"But what about now?" we ask him in unison.

"You will be apart for six months," he answers us. That is what he says. No, that is not all. He also says, "See you in Bangkok." Then his head falls into his plate of spaghetti.

That is it. The Norwegian prophet has spoken across the blue table. I go back to California with Caron. We are apart for close to six months while Jeffrey stays on to make a film for Swedish Television. I live with Jeffrey's mother in California until he returns. Jeffrey writes me long letters. He tells me he is a new man. He has changed. His feet are on the ground now.

"What ground?" I ask him across the blue divide.

Jeffrey returns to California after nearly six months, and we try to pick up the pieces. He finally gets a job with the California Parole Department. Having made a training film for the department a few years earlier, he is now hired on a temporary basis. We move back to Los Angeles. We sleep for a while on a friend's living room floor. We move back to the City of Dreams.

So here we are back in Los Angeles, waiting for Jeffrey to turn thirty-seven. We live in a little rented house on Kagel Canyon Street with the hallway so narrow we have to walk sideways and a backyard with no grass. I decide to go back to college. Caron has turned two, and they tell me that she has to be potty-trained to go to nursery school.

"She is trained," I lie to them.

I warn Caron, "I'll kill you if you poop in your pants." It works. She is trained. That's psychology for you: say what you mean, and mean what you say. I'm ashamed to say it out loud. My God, I am brutal.

I get my degree in psychology, and I get a job in the Probation Department. I become a probation officer. I'm the most unlikely probation officer in the universe. I'm a prude, for God's sake. I'm Mr. Rogers in a skirt. I don't walk on black lines for fear of kissing a Negro.

I drive at five in the morning to Juvenile Hall. I drive on the freeway with a near-empty tank and a full bladder to keep awake. Last night, I worked till midnight because the kids had decided to break their boredom with a minor riot of sorts. They beat the shit out of one another, and then they smeared their own bodily waste on the beige walls. They even pushed a few turds under the door for us to admire. It stank to high hell in the halls.

They pushed the beds against the doors so the officers couldn't enter the rooms. We had to call in the sheriffs to help out. After several hours of futile pleading and vain threats, the kids finally came out, smiling sheepishly. At last growing hungry enough, they came out for milk and cookies. A few of the juvenile offenders and one of the probation officers had to be taken to the hospital. Several of the kids were put in the infirmary on the premises, and some of the serious agitators were placed in isolation for the night.

This early hour, driving from Arleta on the 5 Freeway toward downtown, I wonder to myself how in the world this mess had happened. Is this the undertow? Is this what we are reduced to: shit on the walls? Rats in a maze finger painting with their own shit? I see it all too clearly through the fog on the freeway at five in the morning.

The first day on the job, on probation myself as a newly hired probation officer, I hear one of the officers yell at the kids, "Line up, you motherfuckers." I stand awkwardly to the side by myself, not knowing what to say or do. With a huge ring of keys attached to my belt, I look somewhat official. But I have never encountered that word before: *motherfuckers*. What does it mean? I close my eyes for a second. I swallow my Danish tongue deep in my throat, and I whisper, "Please, line up."

I wait. I hold my breath. I wait for them to roll on the floor with laughter. I wait for them to walk away. This will be my last hour, I think. The kids stare at me. Slowly they begin to line up. They take pity on me. "Please" is not a word in their vocabulary. The more I say "please," the more they line up. I feel myself reeling them in.

We stare at one another across the space that divides us. We are strangers. But we know that we have met once before at the still point. We have met where repulsion becomes love. I see the moment trapped deep in their eyes. We have touched hands at this point before.

"Look valiant. Act generous. Be fearless," the ghosts on the other side of the space that divides us whisper. "Be thoughtful.

Be stoic. Be straight. Stand tall. Be silent." I hear the voices floating above the holy ground between us.

"Your hair is like a doll's hair," Jasmine tells me, reaching out for me.

Jasmine, a big black girl, wants to touch my hair. Jasmine has been raped and beaten by her father, her brothers, her uncles, and, she tells me, by the cops, too. Her knees are scarred in a grill pattern from kneeling on the floor heater while her brother and his friends raped her up the ass with the wooden handle of a plunger. Her layered stomach and her massive breasts are dotted with the hollow remains of cigarette burns.

Her lovely name is the only blessing bestowed on her in seventeen years of life. Jasmine has never owned a doll. She has never sat down at a table for a real meal. She has never slept in a clean bed. Juvenile Hall is as close to anything she can call home. She is Tuesday's child with no Wednesday ahead. Her scarred cheek, slashed years ago by a mean knife, has never been stroked by a loving hand.

"Are you for real, miss?" Jasmine asks me.

"I hope so, sweetheart," I answer her. I look into her big brown eyes. I say "sweetheart." She is huge and ugly, and she smells nothing like the sweet promise of her name. She smells of rot and waste. She is what you run away from if you meet her on the street. I say "sweetheart," and I have her in the palm of my hand. I see Jasmine in my hand.

Jasmine's hair looks like the quills on a hedgehog. The black has turned orange at the ends from being straightened with a hot iron and Vaseline. I smell a faint burned smell when I'm near her. I have heard the other kids call her "big yellow heifer." I understand, somehow, that they call her "yellow heifer" because she is light-skinned.

I'm not sure what *heifer* means. I look it up in the dictionary. Heifer: as in *heahfore*, a young cow that has not borne a calf. At least they don't call her a "yellow bitch." She would pummel them if they did. I would have to lock her up in isolation, and it's not easy to drag a furious monster twice your size into isolation. I would have to call for help. Three big male guards and I would have to sit on top of her to calm her down.

"Please" doesn't work when you are out of control with rage. "Please" never works when you see the green eye of the Dragon. The rage lifts up the universe and tosses it like a pink ball against the yellow wall. I know the rage. It becomes the shit on the wall.

I look up *motherfucker* at the same time. It is not listed there in *Webster's New World Dictionary*. Motherfuckers don't exist. What do you know?

"You're a fool, miss. But I like you," Jasmine says with a big grin. I don't know what to say. I want to cry. But I know that's not a good idea. Instead I say, "Thank you, sweetheart. I know I'm a fool, and I like you, too." Jasmine and I know each other. We have met before at the still point where the rage comes face-to-face with love.

Now, it's Jasmine's turn to look as if she is going to cry. But she doesn't, of course. She knows better. The two of us look at each other. I stroke her hair. I look at my palm, and I see ashes in my hand. My hand is filled with the ashes from Jasmine's hair.

I smell the burned fragrance of Jasmine in my hand, and I see that I didn't know that I had lived in paradise all this while. I see her in my hand while I wait for the prophecy by the drunken Norwegian to come true.

What now? Where is Bangkok? Where is the Star of David? Jeffrey hates his work with the Parole Department. It is killing him. Then, he comes home from work one day when he is thirty-seven. He looks at me and says without blinking, "I'm quitting. I want to open up a gallery."

"A gallery?" I ask him. "What do you know about a gallery? And must I remind you that we have no money."

"We have four thousand dollars from my retirement fund. We can use that money," he suggests in a tentative voice. "It's my dream to work and live with books and photographs."

"What about Caron and me?" I question him. "What about me? How do I fit in?" I don't tell him that I think he is a dreamer and a gambler in life. I don't remind him that I shouldn't have to point out his shortcomings over and over again.

"We'll manage. Don't we always manage?" he answers me with a little tone of doubt behind his voice.

I finally agree. I know that he is dying. Jeffrey has become a man with no hope and no promise. I agree that I will keep working with the Jasmines of the world for a while longer. We will live off of my income. It's only fair. It's a leap of faith for both of us. But it doesn't feel like a matter of choice. We do it. We jump into the world of commerce and art feet first with our eyes shut.

"Sink or swim," they say. Sink or swim. A year later, I quit my job. I am not made to be a probation officer. I'm good at counting the kids in line, and I'm good at lining them up. But I will cut out my tongue before I say "motherfuckers" out loud.

I join Jeffrey at the gallery. I know nothing about photography. But I believe that the art world can't be that different from Juvenile Hall. When reduced to the basic ingredients, the manure of life smells the same coming out of any of us. I have seen for myself that you can smear one kind of shit or the other on the walls. Who can tell the difference?

Life is a willful performance, I remind myself, looking at the ashes in my hand. I can deal with that. I know now how to count my blessings. I'll count my blessings while I look at artists expressing themselves everlastingly. If the artists think they have something to say, it's fine by Jasmine and me.

Jeffrey and I manage to listen each minute and every hour of the day. Dead or alive, artists yap in our ears for fifteen years: "Hang my picture here. No, not there. I want to raise my prices. You're not selling enough of my work. I want a show. I'm different. I've things to say to the world. Why do you show more of his work than mine? Why is my work in the bottom drawer?"

"Give me a break," I say while we float along, in, and around La Cienega Boulevard the best we can. We paint the walls. We vacuum the carpets. We hammer in the nails. We lick stamps. We lick and lick. We send out press releases. We mail out invitations by the carload. We frame photographs. We do endless exhibitions. We pack and ship. We serve cheap champagne in plastic glasses. We smile. We kiss and kick ass. We deal with turkeys in bow ties taking furious notes and calling themselves museum curators. We never sleep. We entertain. Our lives are six degrees of separation from the abyss. We climb the walls. We are always in debt.

We have Suzanna along the way. She is my gift to myself. She is my angel child. She comes twelve years after Caron. Suzanna doesn't get potty-trained at the age of two. Suzanna doesn't get dragged off to Sweden in an ice cold yellow Volkswagen bus. I never tell Suzanna, "I'll put my head on the pillow of snow and dream of fire."

Hiding behind a blustery tone, I was not mistaken when I first told Jeffrey, after joining him at the gallery, that I could deal with the art world my own way. Scratch an artist and a petulant juvenile delinquent oozes out. She oozes out with a faint burned smell. She stands there with her hands on her big hips. She tries to stare me down. I say "please," and she waits her turn. Then, I feed her milk and cookies.

I swing back and forth on my swing. It creaks. I hear it squeak, "Don't whine. Don't bitch. Balderdash. Balderdash." I hear it say, "The world cares diddily squat if you want to express yourself. Don't be crybabies. Don't be wimps. Don't be bores. Balderdash. Balderdash."

I have opened the steel door with the key. The stench of human lives has greeted me floating out from the gray cement walls. I have seen the twelve feet by twelve feet of holy space filled with the world's garbage. I've stretched across the garbage and grabbed my gold ring.

At last, we are free. Jeffrey and I have made it for now. We have snatched the ring together. We sold our photography collection to a Japanese museum when a small window of opportunity opened up, fifteen years after Jeffrey started the gallery. We had bet on the right horse. We made it with a share of decency. We did not trample on the needy. We remained forever mindful.

Am I for real? Am I a fool? "Yes, Jasmine, I'm a real fool," I whisper to her in my hand. "I'm as foolish as they come. I'm as real as you. I'm as real as the ghosts across the table."

I see the ghosts all too clearly through the fog on the freeway at five in the morning. Oh, Jasmine, the sweetest flower in the palm of my hand.

CHAPTER 13

"So, you're going to be a granny," she speaks to me with the little smile of hers. I stare hard and cold at her across the table. My eyes warn her that her teeth show like the grin of the Cheshire cat. I take a sip of my Bombay Sapphire gin martini, up with a twist of lemon. Oh, the clear blue taste of sapphire.

I answer her in the little voice of mine, "I guess so." I think to myself while I take another sip of my martini that I haven't really thought about myself that way. Granny. Granny. Granny. It has a horrible sound.

"And," she says through the teeth shimmering across the table, "you're going to be the granny of a set of twins. Congratulations."

I smile the little smile of mine. I don't answer her. I'm cooler than cool. Does the Cheshire cat know that she is on the same slide as I am? Does she realize that the most amusing trick on the slide is that you can fall off it in the blink of an eye? Does she understand you can fall off the slide whether you are high or low or just somewhere in the middle?

I smile at the Cheshire cat across the table, chiding myself: "Oh, get over it. She only means to be funny in a sort of intimate way. Grow up. You're not the only granny in the world. The world is full of grannies. The world is full of dead grannies. That's what happens when you are lucky: you grow up to be a granny. Shame on you. Get a grip. Sooner or later, we all slide down the big slide."

Twenty-seven years ago, I saw Alice, my mother-in-law, far down the slide. I saw from the distance that she was not

Naomi from the Old Testament, and I was not her Ruth, the daughter-in-law, who said to her in a devoted voice: "Whither thou goest, I will go." I didn't want to follow Alice down the same path on the slide. I wanted to find my own way. Only for as long as I was able did I try to please her. Then, I lost my will and my desire to be her dutiful servant.

I see Alice sitting in my dad's green chair. Ever the hospitable and gracious host, my father lets her sit in his appointed seat. I see Alice's left hand raised up over her head, pulling on a strand of black hair. The back of her head is placed lightly against the headrest. Her small teeth show through her thin purple lips, and her brown cat eyes shine bright below her arched brows. Swinging up and down, her right leg crosses over her left.

Composed and elegant, Alice looks beautiful in his green chair. Her yellow silk blouse flows gently over her black Capri pants. She appears in charge while Egon sits on Putte's hard dining room chair at the table. Perry, the bird, is dead. My mother has been dead for close to five years, and I sit on the chair next to my father.

Alice, Caron, and I are on a visit to the old country. After expressing a wish to see my country, Alice paid for the journey by buying the three of us tickets on SAS. Jeffrey stays in California to tend the fires back home. He's struggling to maintain the gallery he has recently opened in a small space on Norwich Court across from the Blue Whale on Melrose Avenue.

Now, I am back in number 25 in Valby, and Alice is sitting in my father's green chair. I see my father appearing thin on Putte's chair at the table. He is not in charge today. The two little lonely bumps on his high bony shoulders show through his light blue shirt. They stick up, one on each side of his big, balding head. Caron plays on the floor with the ring a boy has given her down on the street.

The ring is too large. Caron keeps turning it around her finger. She is six, and the boy is six. He wants to marry her. In his Danish mind, she is a rich American girl. Caron is lovely, and he wants to leave the street, the sooner the better. The boy is ready. They will go to California together where he'll make her happy forever.

After meeting Caron on the street, he flies past number 23, number 21, number 19, down the stone stairs at the end of the block, past the hardware store, around the corner, across the street from the bakery down to the right a few more blocks into the toy store. He buys her a ring with a big red glass stone in the middle. "You will always love me," the boy tries to convince Caron, handing her a token of his love.

Caron turns the ring around her finger. You can slice the air with a knife. Alice speaks English, and Egon speaks Danish. I go back and forth. I try. I swear I try to translate and negotiate between the two of them. I see them, two giant genies squeezed into a tiny bottle that is ready to explode at any second. Alice thinks that my father is an ignorant oaf and a total loser in life. My father thinks Alice is an American stuck-up bitch who looks down upon him.

I try to make them both happy. Who is she, anyway? Who is Alice to gallop into our house? Who is she to make him feel small? Why doesn't she stop looking at him as if he is a piece of shit to be stomped on? Why doesn't she stop?

I see Alice looking at my father as if he is a big ugly turd to be flushed down the toilet. I try, I swear. I try to clear the tension in the room. I try to divert my father's attention the best I can. I tell him charming stories that I grab out of the air. I tell him of the large onion fields in California. "They bring tears to your eyes as you pass them in the car. They have no end in sight."

I tell him about the salad dressing made of blue cheese and about the oranges that hang off the trees. "They are big and juicy. You can pick them right off the trees and eat them."

I tell him about the mountains. "During the summer, they have caps of white snow. You can see the snow on a clear sunny day."

I tell him about the swimming pools. "They cascade blue water over the side of the green hills. The pools are built right to the edge of the hills in California."

I tell him about the palm trees. "They sway like hula girls. They grow as tall as the Round Tower in the center of Copenhagen."

I tell him about the heat. "It melts you like butter. You seep into the pavement, leaving only a wet pool as a sign of your former self."

I tell him all that comes to mind. I want him to be happy, but all I see are his eyes bulging with rage while he inhales his Cecil. Gray smoke flows through his nostrils. Her brown cat eyes stare at him through the smoke. I see Alice's eyes sneer at him: "Go away, you shit. Go back to your shit."

Alice's eyes shine: "You're nothing. You're nothing. You have always been nothing. You look like shit. You will always look like shit. You are deader than dead shit. You are dust like the color of your huge ugly head. You are dust."

Caron looks at her beautiful granny. Caron loves her granny. Alice is fun. She is more fun than her mother. Alice waves her hands with nails the color of lilac through the gray smoke coming out of Egon's nose. I see her brown eyes mock him: "You piece of shit."

The genies are out of the bottle, thrashing each other over the head. Their bodies swell up, filling the room in number 25 in Valby. Caron and I shrink beneath their shadows. I want to creep under the carpet and hide for the rest of time.

Egon coughs. He feels better when sitting up in the chair and holding his head high. He doesn't mind sleeping in his chair at night. Alice, Caron, and I sleep in my parents' bedroom, where the cracked mirror has been replaced. I see the child in the mirror. I see her sad.

While we sleep in his bed, my father's skinny white legs take heavy steps down the brown linoleum stairs, down the stone stairs at the end of the block, past the hardware store, around the corner, into the bakery. He buys cinnamon snails with white sugar glaze spread thick on top and croissants covered in deep dark chocolate.

He walks back home. He walks up the stairs into the kitchen. He can't breathe. He pours hot water over the ground Kenya coffee beans. He brings out the fine china from behind the first door in the cabinet: Royal Copenhagen the color of yellow cream, patterned with muted red and green flowers.

My father sets the table: four plates, four cups, and four white cloth napkins. He sits down on Putte's chair at the table. The large crossword puzzle from the back of the Sunday paper is spread out in front of him. He looks at the squares through the round magnifying glass in his right hand.

He waits, working the crossword puzzle while we sleep. No more yelling at Pia from the green chair: "Go get the rolls."

No more yelling: "Go get the milk." No more yelling: "Go get the cigarettes." He waits patiently for the Queen Mother, the Queen, and the Princess to wake up.

The Princess wakes first. She opens the door. She looks at her grandfather, who waits at the table set in Royal Copenhagen china. She sees him at the table smoking his Cecil. One of his steel-blue eyes looks bigger than the other through the magnifying glass.

Caron sits down across from him. Egon stares over the cream-colored dishes with the muted flowers at the girl with the straw-colored hair. Sitting small on the chair, she reminds him of someone. Her back is straight, and she wears her favorite blue blouse. He hands her the croissant covered with deep dark chocolate.

He pours the coffee into her cup. Caron's eyes grow bigger than saucers. He pours lots of hot milk into the coffee. She is in heaven. He reminds her of no one. She sees only a big gray man across from her. They don't speak. They can't speak. She loves her grandpa. He loves her.

Alice wakes up from her sleep. The Queen Mother walks into the living room. No "good morning" to you. No "how are you?" No need for good manners. Alice sees the table set and the fourth chair waiting for her. No "how nice of you to make breakfast."

Alice looks at Egon instead. She hates his old smell. She is disgusted. What does she care for Royal Copenhagen china? It looks comical and stupid on the table in number 25 in Valby. He is disgusting. We have to leave today. She can't stand him a day longer. She can't stand him.

I'm sick to my stomach. Please, be nice, Alice. Please, be nice,

Dad. Caron sees nothing. She loves her grandma. She loves her grandpa. He feeds her croissants covered with dark chocolate. I see brown chocolate crumbs falling down her chin.

We pack up. We walk down the stairs. We walk through the park. We see the empty field on our right. Through the tunnel we walk. We take the train at 8:10 in the morning four stops to the Central Station. We leave my father sitting in his green chair to die alone two years later. He can't breathe in his chair. His breath is gone.

We move into a small room in a grand apartment that has seen better days on Vesterbro Steet. It smells of cabbage. Alice and I share the bed. Caron sleeps on the floor. Alice is happy. She sings in a high voice. She rents a car. We are going to the country to visit my mother's family. We are going to the islands. We are on our way to the country.

We pick up my dad. He stands in his best gray suit in front of number 25 waiting on the street for us to arrive. He wears his light blue shirt and the blue tie with red stripes. His gray fedora sits smartly on his head. He is dapper. He will drive. He knows where we are going. He knows the way.

My father is larger than the orange Volkswagen bug that Alice has rented. I sit in the front seat next to him. I'm the guide. I read the map while Alice and Caron sit in the back seat.

We are on our way to the country. The oats wave yellow in the gentle breeze. The cows moo aloud in the green grass. The birds sing in the blue sky above. I point, bubbling over with joy: "Look, those are my yellow fields. They are all mine. Look at that yellow house. That's my yellow house. Look at that rose-colored cottage. That's my cottage.

"Look at the white and pink hollyhocks growing high up the walls of the cottage. They are all mine. Look at that fairy tale castle. That's my castle. Those are my cows. That's my big farm. That's my white church there. Those are my oak trees. That's my blue sky, too."

I'm happy. I am busy pointing, and I forget to look at the map. We're lost. My father is dressed to the nines, and he can't bear being lost in front of Alice. He yells, "We are lost."

"So what?" says the Queen Mother, cool and collected. My father stares at me. I see his eyes turn black. The paw lands on the red mark left on my face from childhood. Smack. My father's hand lands in a sudden smack on my cheek. My eyes grow big. "Stop the car. Stop the car," yells Alice. He stops the car.

The car stops in a sudden jerk. We tumble out of the car onto the road. "Look at that country road," I point. "It's all my road." Alice shoves him through the door into the back of the car next to Caron. He is quiet. Alice drives. She is in charge.

Caron looks ashamed that she loves her grandpa's chocolate croissant. Her big eyes look away from her grandpa out the window at the blue sky. Alice drives the orange Volkswagen bug to the train station. I look away from him out at the country road. "Get out. Get out," Alice yells at him. I hear her shouting even though she doesn't use these words: "Take the train back to your green chair. You old shit. You shit."

CHAPTER 14

No one ever measures up. Today in the *Los Angeles Times*, I read that a person's blood pressure may be set in the womb before birth. The article goes on to state that fetuses with shorter thighbones have higher readings of blood pressure as children. I ask myself, "Shorter than what?"

I look at my thighbones, and my pressure reaches the roof. I think to myself that I'll have the doctor measure the twin's thighs immediately at their birth. My God, what they don't know these days. How in the world do they find out these things? Short thighs, and out goes the baby with the bathwater. Out with the baby before it's too late.

It's all too late for most of us to measure the thighbones. It's clearly too late to measure my father's. There's no hope of bringing him back. Alice, Caron, and I drive on. I can find my way now.

We are on our way to Uncle Freddie, my mother's youngest brother, who buries his aquavit bottle in the ground in his backyard. He hides it away from his wife, Aunt Helen, who falls off her bicycle a few years after this visit and cracks her head wide open. Aunt Helen is never the same again after that.

We are on our way to Aunt Helen, who told Cousin Gudrun and Pia when they were nine to face their fears head on. "Go down in that dark cellar and look the monster in the eye," she said, laughing at them because they were afraid to go down to pick up wood for the fire. "Look him straight in the eye," she challenged them. "Always look what you fear straight in the eye. Never turn your back to the monster."

We are on our way to Uno, the big black poodle, who digs up Uncle Freddie's aquavit bottle from the backyard and brings it to Aunt Helen. "Look," Uno barks, wagging his tail. "Look what I found."

We are on our way to Uncle Hans, who is married to my mother's oldest sister, Aunt Polly. Uncle Hans looks like a gypsy in his brown felt hat. Red suspenders hold his brown pants high up upon his substantial stomach. "Always eat before you get hungry," he counsels us, showing off his big paunch while he sticks his thumbs under the red suspenders and pulls them out a bit.

Uncle Hans has not yet given up tobacco. Standing tall, he greets us with a pipe in his mouth, looking like the proud landowner he no longer is. The family knows that Uncle Hans has long ago banned alcohol from his table.

"No more alcohol in this house," Uncle Hans stated some years back, with deep conviction in his voice.

"Can you believe it?" the uncles and Egon asked one another, shaking their heads in disbelief when Uncle Hans first made this new edict known to the family.

We are on our way to Aunt Polly, who has a case of bad nerves and suffers from having been married to Uncle Hans for too many years. She got the shakes when Uncle Hans turned from thinking like a lukewarm fascist to blazing abroad like a red-hot communist. "He's a commie," the townspeople laughed behind his back.

Aunt Polly first started to shake when Uncle Hans began giving all his farmland away to the poor. This newfound generosity came upon him after their firstborn son, Kurt, was struck dead by a train in America. A little while later, Uncle Hans started giving away his money also.

We are on our way to visit Aunt Misse, my mother's second sister, who in her younger days made silent movies come to life by playing the piano at the local theater. Aunt Misse is married to Uncle Oskar, whose nose has grown wider from drink than the Grand Canyon. Uncle Oskar never loses his sense of his place in the world even after he drinks the family money away. "He thinks he is too good for the rest of us," the townspeople laugh behind his back.

We are on our way to Uncle Thor, my mother's older brother, who delves into the dark corners of the family history. He discovers we are mostly farmers. He finds a few boatbuilders and one shipbuilder sprinkled in here and there. He digs up one single bugle player among us. "We are farmers for hundreds of years," he laments.

We are on our way to Cousin Leif, Cousin Jette, Cousin Grete, and Cousin Gudrun. We are on our way to Cousin Leila, Cousin Anders, Cousin Birgit, Cousin Sven, Cousin Nettie, and Cousin Bert. We are finally in Svendborg on the island of Fyn visiting my family.

I see my mother-in-law overshadowing them all as they sit together on the green velvet couch and in the deep chairs in Aunt Helen and Uncle Freddie's rose-colored farmhouse with the thatched roof. Models of ships hang on the wall behind them. I see them raise their seventeen right hands high in the air, greeting Alice with glasses of golden sherry. "Welcome," they greet her.

She waves her hand in the air and raises her perfect eyebrows high. She laughs and talks in a loud voice. I translate as fast as I can. She sits down at the piano, singing on a high note as she bangs away on the piano keys. She comes all the way from California, where the sun always shines, and she plays the piano. They are polite. "She could be worse," they smile at one another across the sherry glasses.

Alice doesn't know that they play the piano better than she does. She doesn't know that Cousin Birgit yodels songs from Norway while playing the guitar almost as well as André Segovia. She doesn't know that my grandfather sent one of my uncles off on a ship with a one-way ticket to Canada at the age of eighteen because my uncle preferred to play jazz rather than going into my grandfather's shipbuilding business. My uncle never returned to Denmark.

My mother tells me that my grandmother longed for the rest of her life for her son who played jazz to drunks in the bars of Ontario. My uncle knew how to play the piano. Then he died alone in Canada. I remember seeing my mother cry when I was about eight. I saw her crying in the kitchen in number 8B when she learned her brother had died in Canada.

I see my mother walking slowly to the piano that stood against the far wall. I hear her playing to herself while singing in her soft voice, "It was a Saturday evening. You promised me to come for certain. But you never came to me." I remember it well.

Alice doesn't know that Aunt Misse played the upright piano in the theater down the street. Alice doesn't know them. She doesn't care to know them. I see the family losing interest in her also. I see them beginning to fidget in their chairs. Slowly becoming aware of my father's absence, they stare at Alice with seventeen pairs of eyes that sit like two little questions marks in each of their faces. Even Uno's eyes look like two question marks. The eyes look back at me.

"Where is Egon?" they ask. "What happened to Egon?" Alice doesn't see them. She is too busy playing the piano. They look around the room. They look in the car. They look under the car. They look at one another. I look down at my hands. Too ashamed to speak out, I can only sigh and whisper, "He's home." Even if making no sense whatsoever, I don't say what I should have said: "Egon has gone back home to die in his green chair. But first Granny ate the wolf."

Does measuring the thighbones make any sense? Does it make sense that I feel remorse because I did not save my father from Alice? Till my last breath, even though Alice saw herself saving me from my father, I shall never be able to forgive myself for my failure to spare him the humiliation of being chewed alive while dressed in his finest.

Should this world of ours always make sense? Did it make sense when I heard the big question that echoed in my father's head: "To be, or not to be?" A mere child hearing the voice of my father's terror, I stood behind him and watched his back bent low in front of the cracked mirror. I did not hear the answer then, and I've not heard it after.

CHAPTER 15

Bangkok may well be the final destination where we all meet again as had been predicted by the drunken Norwegian during the ill-fated Christmas in Sweden. But before we meet up in Bangkok, I have to count the light switches. I have forty-six light switches. Maybe I have more.

I'm the queen of the light switch. I turn it on, and I turn it off. No small matter, this feat. I ask no one when and how to press it. No longer living with my father who waited in the green chair for Pia to come home and disturb him, I'm today the queen of my own light switch.

"What happened?" I ask the ghosts whispering to me across the blue table. My name is now Pea. In the garage I have a new Jaguar the color of green sea frost with white leather interior. It is equipped with air-conditioning, automatic locks, automatic windows, and remote keys with buttons.

I have a media room that also functions as the guest room. I have a closet filled with clothes. I have brown shoes that stand neatly on their shelves. I have black shoes, red shoes, white shoes, rain boots, snow boots, hiking boots, high boots, and low boots. I have winter coats in all colors. I have summer coats. I have fall coats, too. I even have a coat hand painted with chickens.

I have hats. I have felt hats, wool hats, straw hats, blue hats, and red hats. My closet holds an island of drawers that stands in the center filled with socks, silk underwear, and silk scarves in all colors. My closet is the size of the one small room and the one little kitchen of the apartment in number 8B on Queen's Street.

I have my own office. I have two computers. I have an iMac on my desk, and I have one Apple iBook that I just bought to take with me when I fly with my friend to Puerto Vallarta to play and rest at the Hotel Camino Real. On a private beachfront in Mexico, under the shade of straw umbrellas, we will drink endless margaritas while I also listen to music on the headphones of my portable CD player.

I fly to Hawaii. I fly to Japan. I fly to China. I fly to Africa and Australia. I fly to Europe. I fly around the world. Egon and Putte, Uncle Freddie, Aunt Helen, Uncle Hans, Aunt Polly and Aunt Misse, Uncle Oskar, they never flew. Cousin Kurt and Uncle Thor never flew. Cousin Leila never flew. Eleanor, Edy, Egor, Else, and Erik, they never flew. My four grandparents never flew.

I see from my desk the glass door that leads out to the wooden deck with three oak trees shading the outdoor tables and chairs. The trees grow through holes cut into the deck around their trunks. The deck spans the entire house; from it, I can see the sun rising in the east if I wish to get up early enough from my king-size bed.

I see from the deck the lights twinkle in the night across the valley to the San Gabriel Mountains. I see from the deck the orange harvest moon climbing over the mountains. I have a built-in barbeque grill that is larger than my parents' divan. I grill steaks. I grill chicken legs. I grill corn on the cob. I grill peppers and onions and huge mushrooms brushed with olive oil. I see from the front of the house the sun sinking below the hills in the west over the swimming pool shaped like a rock lagoon.

I sleep in a white-upholstered king-size bed that faces a television set the size of our dining room table in numbers 8B and

25. I sleep on an extra-high mattress and goose-down pillows. I have four bathrooms including one for Honey the cat.

I have two glass showers with two showerheads each. I have a bathtub that seats two with six Jacuzzi faucets to turn on at my whim. I have four white porcelain toilets, with white seats to sit on. I have five white porcelain sinks. I have a double stainless sink in the kitchen. I have a matching white washer and dryer standing next to each other in their own room. I have an electric iron that I never use.

I have tile pavers that stretch in the color of sand over the living room floor and across the kitchen and dining room floors as well. I have a huge fireplace in the living room with gas logs that turn on without anyone having to kindle the wood. I have a palm tree plant in the living room that reaches the ceiling, where eight skylights face the blue sky above.

I have three skylights in the kitchen. I have a wine cooler filled with two hundred bottles of red and white wine. I have a husband whose office is larger than the entire apartment in number 25 in Valby. His desk, made of granite, sits high like a throne in the castle.

I have speakers that play music throughout the house, inside and out. I control the sound from the stereo equipment centrally placed in the family room. I have hundreds of CDs that I play on two CD players. I have two tape players. I have two DVD players. I have a family room with a television the size of Denmark.

I have a glass door that leads to a small Japanese garden off the kitchen on one side. Another glass door leads from the office into the same garden. We open the doors, and we meet for lunch. We sit at a small wooden table and eat our tuna fish sandwiches with pickles. We hear the water babbling softly out of the pipe made of yellow bamboo into the small water fountain. I have my own palm trees that sway in the golden sun.

I have black-and-white and color photographs. I have paintings on the wall. I have more books than lined the shelves in the library where I spent my childhood looking at the pictures in "The Princess and the Pea" while I waited for my mother to pick me up. I have an electric gate that is remote controlled by the switch on the telephone.

I have an alarm system that keeps strangers out of my empire. I have an intercom system. I have two purebred Japanese dogs: Oscar, who is black, and Daisy, who is white. I have a stainless steel refrigerator filled with milk, butter, juice, jam, bread, lettuce, steak, cheese, beer, white wine, Coca-Cola, pickles, mayonnaise, lettuce, and tomatoes.

I have four burners in an island of brown granite in the center of the kitchen. I have a stainless steel microwave oven above the stainless steel convection oven. I have Italian cookbooks, French cookbooks, and Mexican cookbooks stacked behind glass doors in the cabinet in the kitchen. I have a kitchen table made of glass surrounded by four chairs covered with pictures of floating angels woven into the beige cloth.

Through the glass door of our wood cabinets built into the walls I see more dishes and glasses than were in all the kitchens of numbers 8B and 8A before they burned down. I have a dining room with a table large enough to squeeze in twelve for the Thanksgiving turkey. I have original Frank Gehry cardboard chairs from the '70s.

I have six black telephones with three lines each. I have DSL. I have e-mail. I have a fax machine. I have two printers plus two extra ones stored in the garage. I have two scanners. I have gas heat and cool air flowing through the ducts as needed from on top of the red-tiled roof. I have five huge garbage cans below the garage. I have patio furniture in all directions. I have a housekeeper who keeps it all clean.

I count the light switches. I'm doing inventory. I count. I take score. I'm taking note. I keep track. At the pearly gates, I want to be sure to measure up. When there, I am sure to gauge the line in front of me. Who among us gets to have eternal life? Who among us will suffer everlasting disgrace?

I want grace. I evaluate the situation: what story to tell? Should I tell the "poor-little-me" tale or the other one? I make a good guess. When I see St. Peter stroking his white beard, I hand him the list that stretches far down the steps of Jacob's ladder to the stone of Bethel. It stretches at least 10 rods that measure up to 60 cubits or 120 spans or 360 handpalms or 1440 fingers in length.

"Are the thighbones long enough?" I ask him in my humble voice. "You did read the article in the health section in the *Los Angeles Times*, did you not?" Sure that he must have seen it, I beseech St. Peter with questions.

"It was in there Monday, August 19, 2002, on page S3," I tell him. I see that he looks a little befuddled. I don't mean to confuse him or upset him. I just want him to remember the part about the length of the thighbones and high blood pressure.

"I haven't been the most easy-going of persons," I say in my downcast voice. I know that I haven't been as patient as I should have been in life. But I want to remind him that he could just as easily blame my thighbones as me if he so chooses.

St. Peter looks me up and down. "Even though you could

have been somewhat less selfish, you're not as bad as some," I hear him thinking out loud. "By all accounts, you're hardly the most perfect among them. You are not exactly what we call 'salt of the earth.'"

"I can't deny it," I whimper. "I know that I am a loyal Dog only when it suits my selfish leanings." I say this to remind him that Dogs are also honest and generous creatures. I want to tell St. Peter that Jeffrey has been my Tiger in life. St. Peter must know that Dogs and Tigers are made for each other.

I think he needs to know that Jeffrey has been my protector. I also want to tell him that Jeffrey has been my warrior, my confessor, and my sweetheart through the years. "If you would like a list, I can write it in a hurry," I try to convince him.

"It's no trouble at all," I push on. I want St. Peter to remember Jeffrey in a good light when his time is up. I want to remind him that Jeffrey has the Star of David in his hand. I wish St. Peter to see how much I appreciate my good luck. I wish him to know that I recognize the moments when good fortune fell into my lap.

St. Peter should know that I'm grateful for having had Jeffrey in my life. With only Jasmine in my hand, I am thankful to have had Jeffrey by my side. I realize that she is not the Star of David by any means. "But Jasmine is not nothing, is she?" I ask him.

"She is not nothing?" I ask him again, hopeful that St. Peter will appreciate my honest attempt, however limited to a double negative question, at making something out of Jasmine. "But," I implore him, "in case you don't see her my way, then tell me quickly so I will not fall into everlasting disgrace on the other side without Jeffrey. Please, be frank with me."

I coax him on. "I can write you a list of all of Jeffrey's failings just as easily." Being the selfish Dog that I am, I tell St. Peter without hesitation that I don't want him to let Jeffrey fall into a place where I am not invited. I don't want Jeffrey to have eternal life without me. It is also of grave importance to me that St. Peter hears that I have walked on the path next to Jeffrey without a leash. "I have my own way," I press upon him.

"So," says St. Peter.

I can see he is losing patience with me. So I shut up and don't tell him that I can honestly say that I have never turned my back on the monster. I don't tell him that I never called anyone a motherfucker. I don't tell him that I have looked the Dragon straight in the eye even when I wanted to cower like the Dog with my tail between the legs. Not wishing to irritate him anymore than I already have, I decide not to remind him that life is not a dance on roses.

We stand silent at the gate together, St. Peter and I. "Your way is made of sugar and spice," he finally drones, "but then again, you are not the worst I've seen." He cries in his beard, complaining, "Judging people is a trying job."

I begin to feel a little sorry for him. But while I see that he doesn't have an easy life, I think to myself that St. Peter could be a little less trite. Thank God, I'm smart enough not to speak my mind. I wasn't born yesterday, you know. St. Peter hesitates for a second, pulling on his white beard. Then he says, "But we can't be too choosy, I have been told from above."

I hear him sighing to himself. "Yes, very well, you're in. You are in," St. Peter finally roars as he bangs his gavel on the clouds.

I cross the threshold to heaven. St. Peter roars down to the woman behind me, "You're out." I hear him yelling as he points his long finger toward the woman named Lisbeth who is following in my footsteps, "You think you look just like the one ahead of you, but you're nothing like her."

Somehow St. Peter must have knowledge that at one time my parents had debated whether to name me Lisbeth or Pia– and that in the end they chose to toss poor Lisbeth out on the street. I guess St. Peter knows even the most trivial of matters. Of course, again, I say nothing.

I hear him stammer at Lisbeth with the voice of the Furies, "You...you...you good-for-nothing outcast. You depraved, ungrateful hag. Go...go back to the street. How...how dare you even climb up here. Sh...sha...shame on you. Shame on you."

I feel a little sorry for her, just as I did for St. Peter a moment ago. Poor Lisbeth behind me, she never had a chance in life after my parents rejected her. All she ever wanted in life was my Christmas goose. Or did she just want to cook it?

Tidal waves beat the street again and again until they wash away the gray coat. They wash away the pink and the blue rubber balls. They wash away the brown schoolbag, the curry-colored chairs, the onions, the grocer, and the baker. They wash them all away. They wash away the green hat. They wash away the piano. They wash away Jasmine. The lights are off.

CHAPTER 16

Like magic, she wakes up with young pointed breasts. Her hair shines golden and silky down her back. Like magic, the gap between her teeth closes its gate, and the brown freckles on her nose vanish into the velvet of her creamy skin. She is thirteen today.

Pia looks at her own reflection in the mirror. She sees the same nose that the boy living below her punched a year ago. She had told him then, "You're a brat. Your brother is a brat, and your mother is scum." He punched her in the nose a year ago, and today she is thirteen with the same broken nose.

She sees the same flat chest she saw there yesterday. She sees the same yellow hair and the same huge gap. She sees the same brown freckles on the nose. With the crack in the mirror running through her reflection, she sees that there is no magic to turning thirteen.

Pia sees her mother behind her reflection. Wearing the green hat, she stands short and round and missing a front tooth. Her mother's hazel eyes look faded in the mirror. She sees her mother put the right hand up over her mouth to cover her shy smile. She sees her mother's tired eyes behind the thick glasses, loving her.

Her mother takes a step toward Pia. She places her mouth on her daughter's cheek and kisses it gently. "Happy birthday," says her mother, blowing spit at her just a little. "Psst psst." Her mother purses her lips with the superstition of the Chinese mother who, in hopes of keeping the evil spirits away, dismisses her bouncing baby boy and declares, filled with feigned shame, that he's merely a useless girl.

While her mother's "psst psst" tells her she is a useless girl, the hazel eyes tell her that she is her mother's beautiful daughter. They say, "You are my tall, blond daughter. You are my princess. You are my glory and my pride. You are the best of me."

Pia sees the open space in front of her mother's mouth. She turns away from her mother and looks into the mirror again. She sees the black crack running through her. She sees the pleasure in the hazel eyes behind her. She sees that she is beautiful.

Pia is thirteen today. She is not her mother behind her. She is herself. She is in luck. She loves her mother for loving her. She's ashamed of her mother for being her mother. She is ashamed of herself for being ashamed of her mother.

"Why do you always wear that green hat?" Pia whines. "Why do you put your hand over your mouth when you smile? Why don't you fix that tooth? Why don't you wear a brassiere?" She hates her mother's nipples showing through her brown dress the way they do.

Pia is ashamed of her own thoughts. Why are you so fat? Why is your nose so large that you can put two fingers up your nostril? Why are your shoes old and ugly? Why is your hair so dull? Why are you my mother?

Happy in the knowledge that she will never grow ugly and old and dull, Pia looks at herself in the mirror. Behind her reflection she sees her mother lift a brown box from the floor. "Here, Pia, here is your birthday gift."

Pia turns around and looks in the box. "Oh, my God," she bursts out, seeing the complete set of Jalna books by Mazo de la Roche, bound in beautiful red leather. All her dreams lie jam-packed in a measly brown box.

"Oh, Mommy." She grabs her mommy and hugs her. Her beautiful adorable little mommy. She loves her mommy to the moon. She will put the Jalna books right between *Call of the Wild* and *Lady Chatterley's Lover*.

"My own set bound in red leather," Pia squeals, jumping up and down. She smells the leather. She loves the people who live in the house of Jalna. They know how to live in the house of Jalna.

They will live right here on the shelf below the row of Suzy books. Suzy has red hair that flows behind her when she rides her Icelandic pony with the speed of light on the path through the beech woods. Suzy's father is a forester, and her mother stays home in a little white cottage.

"Oh, Mommy, you are the best," Pia cries out, kissing her mommy a thousand times over and over again. Life will never get any better than this. The joy of it all, she thinks to herself on her thirteenth birthday.

Just a year ago, when only twelve, she remembers it well: Pia walks down the street. She walks from the small minigolf course with the thirty holes on the corner of Vigerslev Road. She carries her golf club in her right hand. She owns her own golf club. The club is perfection. It has a short wooden handle with a metal head turning just a little at a slight angle.

Pia earns the money to pay for the club by delivering newspapers. She carries newspapers in the snow on her blue bicycle, and she runs up and down the stairs to put the papers on the mats in front of the doors. Earning the money by babysitting Hanne's boy, she pays off twenty crowns a month for her blue bicycle.

Henning is only two years old in number 21. Pia babysits him day and night because Hanne is too busy working and dancing to take care of her little Henning in number 21. While Hanne is off, Pia feeds him cream-of-wheat with cinnamon and butter early in the morning.

Pia dresses him in his beige coat and the red scarf. She walks him to the nursery school around the corner not too far from number 25. Henning hangs on to her neck when she kisses him goodbye. He screams and cries for her not to go away. "Pia, don't leave me here," he screams. The schoolmistress slaps her face because she doesn't know how to let go of Henning. She tries hard to be his mommy when she is only twelve years old.

She polishes the bicycle till it shines like a blue diamond. Keeping it out of the rain as much as she is able, she pulls it down the stairs to the shed in the basement in number 25. She locks it with a lock through the spokes on the back wheel. She keeps it dry and shiny while waiting for the sun to come out again.

Today, she walks from the minigolf course down the street past the gray concrete buildings of Lykkebo School on her right. She sees the school where, at age fifteen, after spending six days a week for seven years, she surprisingly passes the state examinations to enter gymnasium. She sees the windows open into the beige painted classrooms where she studies Danish and handwriting.

It seems not to matter whether she writes in cursive or square block letters. She has no patience for perfecting the art. "Slant the letters just so. A little to the right. And don't be so messy with the ink," Mr. Nagel scolds her above her head.

She looks at the lines and lowers her head over the paper. She tightens her fingers around the pen, dipping it into the inkwell in the center of the desk. She sees the blue ink splatter across the white page. She curses the ink through her breath.

In the history lessons, she learns by heart the long row of Danish kings and queens: Christian, Frederik, Christian, Frederik, on and on they come and go. "King Christian is dead. Long live King Frederik," they say. Only once, long ago, did they have a queen on the throne. "The Queen of the North," ruling all of Norway, Denmark, and Sweden, Margrethe I died in 1412. Long live the King.

Pia is told that, sooner or later, Princess Margrethe, only a few years older than she, will wear the crown after her father, King Frederik IX, is dead and buried in his tomb next to the other kings and queens in the cathedral of St. Luke in Roskilde. The "royal doors" will open and some voice will declare, "The King is dead. Long live Queen Margrethe II."

Pia learns English and some German in the beige classroom. When Mr. Voldsen asks her during the English lessons to say *the*, she says *je*. "Say *the*," he repeats over and over again. She sees his face turn red with frustration.

"You're such a nuisance," he grumbles, boxing the back of her head. It's impossible for her to put her tongue on the roof of her mouth against her two front teeth while making the *th* sound. "I can't do it," Pia bursts out with anger. "I'm sick of the English and their ways."

The girls are taught to knit socks and crochet pot-holders, and they learn to embroider their initials onto the blue suits they sew for themselves to wear in gymnastics class. In home-making class, Pia likes to go shopping for groceries with a list and a budget: ground pork for the meatballs, white potatoes, milk, butter, flour, and scouring powder. Envying the boys in the woodworking classes, she laughs out loud, "Today you see me shopping for potatoes, but I'm never going to end up a housewife with a budget."

Swinging her golf club back and forth, she sees the gray buildings where the old music teacher chases them out of the classroom. Ready to hit them on the head because they sing out of tune to tease him, Mr. Nielson raises his violin bow high in his hand. The hairs on the bow flap loose in the air. Mr. Nielson fumes at the mouth as he runs down the hallway with strands from the horse's tail dancing in front of his eyes.

She sees the gray concrete building where she likes learning the order of the Pythagorean theorem in geometry class from Mr. Dannesø, who also teaches them the geography of the land. "Denmark has no mountains," he tells them, as if they don't already know it.

"We have no natural resources. We have only cows and butter and the wind," he says, stressing the sorry facts to them. They learn that they have one lone hill to take pride in. It rises a mere 482 feet above sea level in Jutland. But naming it Skymountain, the Danes exhibit their famous sense of humor about all things in this world.

She sees the gray buildings where, in Bible class, she admires God's powers to stretch out the northern sky and hang the earth in empty space. She wonders how He manages to do it. She imagines God making Adam by breathing life into the dust, and she sees God taking a rib out of Adam and making Eve. She likes the story of Adam and Eve eating the red apple in the Garden of Eden naked in front of the serpent. Then, disappointed, God is sorry He made them, and He decides to send them out into the world to suffer alone.

She likes the story of Noah and his family and the twin birds and the twin beasts spending one hundred and fifty days and one hundred and fifty nights together in one ark before the waters drain away. She wonders where the water goes. She is amazed that Noah, who is at least five hundred years old, builds his ship three stories high, 300 cubits in length, 50 cubits in breath, and 30 cubits in height.

How do they all keep dry? And how do they eat their food in the darkness of the ark while torrents of rainwater fall upon their heads for forty days and forty nights before they come to rest on Mount Ararat? She is amazed that Noah puts only one small window in the ark and places next to it a door sealed by God himself from the outside. She can't believe that the water rises at least twenty-two feet over the surface of the whole earth.

She wonders how Cain found the east of Eden after he slays his brother Abel in the field. She worries about the curt answer Cain gives God when He asks him where his brother is: "I know not; am I my brother's keeper?" Then God marks Cain to safeguard him on his long journey. How far into the east did Cain have to wander?

She sees the window on the second floor of the gray concrete building where just this last winter they are caught in the act of throwing balls made from the snow that sits thick on the windowsills. Tossing the snowballs out of the window, they take aim at the hats of the grown-ups who, in their heavy coats and brown leather boots, stand waiting in line for the bus to come to the stop on the street below. The grown-ups feel the snowballs break apart on the back of their heads. "Where did they come from?" they ask one another.

The surprised grown-ups look up. Noticing the kids ducking below the window in Lykkebo School, they march into the headmaster's office to file a formal complaint. The red-faced teacher lines the class up in front of the blackboard. He slaps them one by one. They feel lucky. They know they get less than they deserve.

She sees the gray concrete building where her brother many years hence ends up teaching religion and political theories. Turned communist, he joins the party at the tender age of eighteen. Poul wants his share of the riches of the world. "I know there's milk and honey out there," he pouts to himself.

Pia is sure that her brother turns his thoughts to communal living and sharing of the land when he hears the misdeeds of the upper classes crackling across the waves of his crystal set radio. "Save me," she hears him sigh when he sleeps in his pullout bed in number 25 in Valby. "Save the masses," Poul shouts from the rooftops of Lykkebo School.

On this happy day, carrying her golf club in her right hand, she swings it back and forth. The pattern of green apples spreads across her white dress. She feels the cool cotton swaying around her bare thighs. She hears the flip-flop sound of her wooden sandals against the gray cement. She steps firmly on the black lines, asking herself: "Why should I worry?"

She sees the brown leather strap across her foot. She sees her toes curl over the little ridge of the blond wood of the sandal. The sun shines high in the blue sky above her. She prays as she swings her golf club back and forth: "Please, let me stay like this forever. Please, let me walk with my golf club down the street forever. Glory. Oh, glory. Oh, the joy of it all."

She knows that life doesn't get any more glorious than this as she walks down the street past Lykkebo School, swinging her club back and forth by the short handle. She knows the minigolf course like the back of her hand. She hits the ball just so. In it drops. She knows every curve. She knows every move.

She makes thirty holes with one stroke each hole. She takes two at the most. She is the best of all. She likes to count and measure things. She's the master of her own universe. She's the champ.

The place is all hers. Never another soul plays the course. Only the man who runs the course sits in his little shed day after day. Pia sees his ugly fat wife with her greasy black hair coming around from time to time. But mostly he sits in his shed alone.

He tries to touch her breasts that are not there yet. He tries to touch them when she pays him his money. She knows what he wants from her, but she doesn't care. She only cares to be the champ of the universe.

She laughs at him. She knows that he can't hurt her. She knows him. She knows that he is scum. She, on the other hand, is the wind that blows the scum away across the oceans. "Here comes your ugly wife," she laughs at him. She knows that he is a coward while he tries to hold her against the wall of the shed.

"Get away, you ugly pig," Pia laughs. "Oink oink." He oinks as he slinks into his shed behind the counter. She sees the golf clubs that hang on the wall of the shed. But her club does not hang on the wall among them. She takes it home with her. She is the world champ of minigolf.

Pia is the champ. The pig cannot kiss her. She won't let him. She knows what he wants. She stops at the grocery store on the way home. She buys a chocolate frog. She puts her teeth into the frog. She feels the white cream filling flow out on her tongue.

She knows where babies come from. She knows they don't come from frogs. She knows they come from kissing. He cannot put his tongue into her mouth. "No, not ever," she says to herself. No one shall ever put his tongue into her mouth. She is the world champ of minigolf. She is herself. She is perfection.

This later day, I'm twenty-seven. My name is now Pea. I'm no longer the champ. I'm no longer perfection. I'm the mother with flaws. Caron is four. I ask her, "Where do babies come from?" She answers me with no sign of doubt in her sweet voice, "They come out of the wall."

Where did she get that idea? Then I remember. Of course, how stupid of me to forget how Caron could have hit upon such an impenetrable barrier in her young mind. Last week, Jeffrey and I had shown her the film we made of her birth. We had taken the picture off the wall and had projected the film on the bare white space. Of course, babies come out of the wall. Where else? Babies come from frogs and walls. Frogs and walls. Where else do they come from?

My little girl is perfection. She is mine. She is mine alone. I see her first. I lay my eyes upon her first. I love her first. I put my nose down to her cheek. I smell her first. Her blue eyes look up at me. They love me first.

Caron looks at me again when her eyes turn green. She looks at me again when her breasts are barely there. She is ashamed of me. She is ashamed of herself for being ashamed of me. She wants me to stay out of her way. She doesn't want to be reminded that she is ashamed of me.

Why do you wear that horrible orange blouse? Why do you put your hand over your mouth when you talk? Why is your laugh so loud? Why are your shoes so high? Why is your hair so curly? Why are you my mother? Then she walks out the door. What else? That is the way of the wave.

CHAPTER 17

The phone rings. It rings again. I'm in no hurry to answer. "Come to Brotman Hospital right away," the voice on the other end bids. Caron has slipped at school. She is hurt. My heart sticks in my throat. Please, dear God, let her be all right. For God's sake, she is only twelve. She is my firstborn. She is my love.

I don't love Caron less than I love the baby in the crib that stands in blond wood next to the wall papered in pink roses. I don't love her less than my second born, who in three years tells her daddy that she has a spider in her mind when she again acts naughty. You may think I love Suzanna more than Caron. But you are mistaken.

I don't love Caron less than I love the baby who at age four picks her ears off the streets of Portland in Oregon. "I can't feel my ears," Suzanna tells me on a visit during Christmas. "You must have lost them," I jest with her. "You must have lost them in the snow. Come, let's look for them together in the snow on the street."

I don't love Caron less than I love the baby who at age six tells her dad what she wants most in the world. "What do you want for Christmas?" he asks her in Rotorua on the North Island of New Zealand. "I want to pet a baby lion," Suzanna answers him sweetly. "All right," he says. "All right, let's go then. Your wish is my command." I don't love her less than the child who gets to pet a baby lion at a wild animal park in Rotorua on Christmas Day when she is six.

I don't love Caron less than the baby who at age seven looks

117

like Maria Frederike van Reede-Athlone. Posed in a blue velvet cape lined with white ermine in 1755, Maria Frederike now hangs on a wall at the Getty Museum. Even the folds in Suzanna's ears fold like Maria's under the white ribbon with the blue bow in the painting. I don't love her less than the one in the crib whom I call "my angel child." You are mistaken if you think that I love her less than "my angel child."

I don't love her less than the baby who at age eight talks to me about the schoolmate whose mother just yesterday killed herself. "You know, you don't have to worry," I try to reassure her. "I would never kill myself. I love you too much for that."

She answers me, "Good, I know that." Her voice sounds not quite certain.

We sit quietly for a few minutes in the car driving down San Vicente Boulevard toward her school in Santa Monica. "Maybe his mother killed herself because she loved her boy too much. She might have thought he would be better off without her," I think out loud, breaking the silence.

"What do you mean by that?" Suzanna asks me.

"I'm not sure. Give me a few years to come up with the answer," I respond on the way to school when she is eight.

The phone rings. It rings again: Caron, her chin cut open in a fall, is at the hospital. I see empty beds standing in a row against the back wall. It smells of pine and rot. Caron, at age twelve, cries alone on the second white bed. I look down at her. "Yes, you are alive. It's just a deep cut on your chin. You'll live," I tell her.

"Please, Mommy, don't let him do it. Please, Mommy," her green eyes beg me to stop the doctor. "Don't let him stick a needle in my chin."

"But, Caron, he must do it," I warn her. "You can't go around with a huge hole in your chin gaping at the world. What will people think?"

"Please, Mommy, don't let him do it," she begs me again. I see the grim reaper in her eyes. I see in her eyes that I fail her again. I never measure up. I always fail her.

I smell her cheek. Caron is two. She stands naked under the peach tree. Her small body has turned brown from the sun. Her hair shines silky in the morning light. I see through the window with the orange netting her naked body covered in brown garden snails. I hear the flies, caught behind the netting, buzzing against the windowpanes.

I see her lift her brown arm to her mouth. The snails stick their heads out from their little houses. She kisses the snails as they glide slowly down her arm. I see she is lovely. I see her in love with her nakedness. I see her in love with the snails. I wish for her to stay under the peach tree in love. Please, let me not fail her, I pray to myself. She is my firstborn. My love.

I put my nose down to her cheek. I smell the salt on her cheek. I smell that she is four. Caron sits at the low wooden table on her little chair waiting for me to come. "Are you the last child to be picked up?" I ask her after I have just driven at a high speed through the city streets to make it in time. Is it possible that I fail her yet again, running in late through the red front door?

I see the large room covered in blue industrial carpet. Caron sits on her chair alone, looking up at me with her hot, tired eyes. She runs away from me. She screams, hiding under the table, "You're not my mommy. I don't want to go home with you. Where's your hair? My mommy has long beautiful hair. My mommy doesn't have short hair. You're not my real mommy. My mommy has pretty hair. Please, don't take me away with you."

I carry her out into the car. She kicks me, crying her heart out. I tell her over and over again, "I'm your mommy. Can't you tell? I'm your real mommy. I just cut my hair today. Look, it's pretty. Look, I'm still your mommy." She touches my hair. She touches my hair once more. She always touches my hair. I'm not her mommy anymore. She is never sure if I'm her mommy. I fail her again.

I smell her cheek. Caron is five. She makes a drawing of her mommy and colors her mommy's hair green. She wins the prize: twenty-five dollars' worth of new clothes at May Company on Victory Boulevard in the Valley. They laugh. Her mother has green hair. I laugh. I laugh a little. Green hair? Who has green hair? Only a witch has green hair. What color light does she see me in?

I smell her cheek. Caron is still five. It's Christmas on Kagel Canyon Street in Arleta. She wakes early at five in the morning, wanting to open her presents. She knows they wait for her under the tree. Having been told that Santa came down the chimney the night before, she stops, afraid of coming face-to-face with him in the living room. What if Santa is still in front of the fireplace? What then? What if Santa decided not to fly back up the chimney? Caron starts to cry, waking her mommy to hold her hand while she walks down the hallway.

I hold her hand, taking slow steps down the narrow hallway. She bends over and throws up on the mustard-colored carpet. I look down at the carpet. I know by the remains left on the mustard carpet that Caron is afraid to meet Santa Claus in person. I also know that she wants her presents.

"Santa is not real," I tell her. "He is not in the living room. Don't worry." She looks up at me with her large eyes where deep behind the blue I see Santa flying away in the night. "My real mommy told me that Santa comes down the chimney," I see her eyes say. I fail her again.

I put my nose down to her cheek. I smell that Caron is seven. I see myself running from the gallery on North La Cienega Boulevard up to the school, where she sits on her little chair crying. She has just fallen in the yard and broken her new front tooth in half. I look at her jagged tooth. I look at the black streaks of dirt and tears running down her cheeks. Tears roll down my cheeks also. "What can I do?" I ask her. "I gave you beautiful teeth. I gave you all I have. I can't give you another."

Don't be silly, I think to myself. It's only a tooth. It is only a tooth, for God's sake. Get real. She is alive. Defeated, I tell her, "Be brave." I fail her again.

I smell her cheek, and Caron is eight. She walks down Gardner Street with her best friend, Sandi. Caron wears brown pants that she hates to wear. The lunch box made of pale blue metal swings in her right hand. The picture of Benji the terrier dog with his ears raised high at attention is imprinted on the box. She walks to school with a tongue sandwich in her lunch box. She hates her mommy. She hates her tongue sandwich. I fail her again.

I put my nose down to her cheek. I smell that Caron is twelve. I see her eyes the color of green apples looking up at me. Her ears are still too large for her face. The gray skirt hangs above her skinny knees, and the blue uniform jacket falls too short at the sleeves. I see her white shirt not tucked into the skirt and her hair cut short with the pink streak running through it.

She kisses me goodbye in the morning. A few hours later she slips at school, cutting her chin wide open.

I smell her cheek. She is thirteen. Caron and I are parked in my new white convertible Mustang at the 7-Eleven store on the corner of Gardner and 3rd Street. It's early evening. I ask her to run in and buy a carton of milk for dinner. She opens the car door. I lean over the seat to close the door, banging it shut on her middle finger. I hear her scream. I run out of the car. I look at her finger. "Can you move it?" I ask her. "A little," she cries.

"I guess it's all right, then," I tell her, my voice not sounding quite certain. Two days later I take her to Kaiser Hospital on Cadillac Avenue. The finger is broken in two places. I fail her again and again.

I smell her cheek. Caron is fourteen. She can't move her legs. She can't bend her knees. I take her to the hospital. After x-raying her legs, the doctor calls, telling me over the phone: "No physical reasons for her symptoms, ma'am. It's time to take her to the head doctor. It's time to get rid of the crutches."

"Why are you so unhappy?" I cry to her across the blue fold of the Pacific. I hear the waves crash behind me. "Why is it never enough? Why did you move from under the peach tree? Why do I fail you, my love? Why do I always fail you, my heart?"

CHAPTER 18

She walks from number 25 in Valby past number 23, past number 21, past number 19, down the block, down the stairs, through the park, through the tunnel, and up the stairs. She waits for the train to travel four stations to the Central Station. It's a Saturday morning, and Pia has on this day been seventeen for one month and a day.

Turning left out of the station, she walks down Isted Street to Helgoland's Street. She smells urine and old beer. The lights of the street glow softly in the dampness. A young woman staggers out of the bar, her stringy bleached hair falling over her face. Red lipstick smears across the mouth.

Pia turns right on Helgoland's Street crossing to Borgerdyd School. She enters the big black door behind the gate to the left of the building. She sees the bronze bust that stands to the left of the entrance on its stone pedestal with the six-pointed star etched under the name of Svenningsen.

Smelling musty mold, she walks up close to the bust. The broad nose shines in the yellow light that hangs from the ceiling. She is face-to-face with Mr. Svenningsen. She performs the age-old tradition: rubbing his nose. His nose has been rubbed for one hundred and sixty-six years, and no one can explain the reason they do it. The star is also a mystery to her.

Pia sees the square plaque of white marble on the wall across from the big door of the entrance. It says in large block letters at the bottom: THEY DIED FOR DENMARK. On top of the plaque is etched: 1940-1945. She reads the nine names listed below the dates.

Nine former pupils of Borgerdyd School died for Denmark during the five years of German occupation. One of the nine was twenty when he died for Denmark. He barely finished with lining up at Borgerdyd School, and then he died for Denmark.

She turns right up the stairs, walking down the long hallway past the caretaker's apartment to the right. She walks into the gym hall, and she sees that she is late again. Number-one rule of the eight rules of conduct in the Borgerdyd's Book of Rules since 1787 decrees that pupils ought to start their journey to school in due time according to their form of transportation, so that they, without hurry, can arrive at school at the right time.

She sees the lines of 209 boys and 42 girls in the gym hall. The first girl lined up in the hallowed halls of Borgerdyd School in 1957. Six years later, the girls have multiplied to 43. She sees the lines of 251 students singing the morning hymn in 251 high, young voices: "In the east the sun rises...." Pia is number 252.

She sees the little gray songbook with the green spine open to page five in their hands. The sun, drawn in black lines on the cover, rises up over the trees that stand close to a Viking mound. If real—and not a drawing on the cover of a songbook—the grave would hold buried "one of the filthiest among all of Allah's creatures," now a dead Viking who used to roam, plunder, and rape everything in sight. The unwashed and lowly status of the Vikings had thus been fixed on the sacrosanct scale of Allah with the indelicate observation written around 922 A.D. by the Arabic traveler Ibn Fadhlan.

Dressed in his finest wools and bedecked with colossal ornaments of bronze and silver and gold, the Viking dreams in his grave with Thor's hammer tied around his neck. His sword, his ax, his dagger, his horse, his cow, his rooster, his dog, his slave girl, and his old wife lie next to him. In a generous spirit, he brings them all along with him on his ship to Valhalla, where they feast on barrels of red wine, horns of dark ale, loaves of grainy bread, huge slabs of steak, and roasted onions.

Ibn Fadhlan sends a message home about the madmen he encounters, loosely translated to this: What a sorry sight of wild donkeys the Vikings make of themselves. Perfectly built, blond, ruddy, and tall like date palms, they do not wash with soap and water or even wipe themselves after shitting loads of shit, pissing rivers of piss, fucking forward and backward, and stuffing mountains of meat and cheese in their faces with their putrid hands.

They sing on in high, young voices. Pia sees her music teacher, his brown hair falling thick over his eyes, moving his round fingers across the keys on the upright piano that stands in the left corner in front of them. She sees Mr. Bentsen, who later sleeps off his usual hangover while they listen to the opera *Aida*.

Pia sneaks into the line behind sweet Ole, who has a young brown beard growing on his chin. Ole writes in the lining of Bodil's white student cap in blue ink, "I love your thighs." The story goes that Ole kills himself the day after their tenth reunion. Bodil now lives in Minnesota, where she is a French teacher.

She sees her Latin teacher in line. Mr. Saxø stands in front of them singing through yellow teeth that protrude far over his lower lip. During the endless Latin lessons, he talks to them of Caesar and the many battles of the Roman warriors as if they should learn to enjoy the spectacles of warfare.

She sees her French teacher in line with his thin red hair combed close to his head. During the French lessons, Mr. Molbo walks daintily like a girl up to the blackboard, where he writes in white chalk: *"Un Cœur Simple"* by Flaubert. She knows in her heart that Mr. Molbo does not have a simple heart.

She sees her English teacher standing short and stocky in line. Mr. Knudsen reads to them from William Golding's *Lord of the Flies* while they listen in horror. Those kids in the book do not line up and sing, "In the east the sun rises..."

She sees her Danish teacher droopy-eyed. Mr. Finsen's breath smells of sour coffee and stale cigarettes when he talks to them in the morning about Gruntvig and Kierkegaard. "Gruntvig is the nineteenth-century cultural maven of Denmark," he says, sharing a whiff of his breakfast with them. Mr. Finsen also teaches them about Greek Ionic columns and about Herodotus's King Kroisos in the lessons of classical civilization. "Oh, the civility of the Greeks," he exclaims with a faint glow of pleasure in his sleepy eyes.

The students know that the Danes are not civil. They know that the Vikings throw stones. They hurl axes at one another's brains. Their heads split open like red watermelons, and the seeds spread across the land. You find the seeds in the pit of the bog. You find them frozen in golden amber.

Pia sees her geology teacher standing firm and grim in line. During the science lessons, Mr. Larsen lines up shoeboxes filled with stones on his desk. He asks the students, "What do you see here?" Then, hoping for a brilliant answer to come his way, he looks across the room. "Black stones," they respond, with no passion for the subject. "Is that all you can muster?" he yells, tossing the stones at their heads while they quickly duck under the desks.

She sees her history teacher with the little bump shaped like the top of a Viking grave on his bald head. Mr. Thomasen takes them on sightseeing tours of the city. She hears his voice drill on: "Denmark consists of over four hundred islands and one large peninsula we know as Jutland. Cut like a runic stone between two oceans, Jutland proudly mounts the ever-moving border between Denmark and Germany.

"In the beginning, Copenhagen was a mere hamlet on a soppy piece of land on the island of Zealand. A few huts facing north and slightly to the east across the narrow strait of water to Sweden was all that Copenhagen was until 1167, when Archbishop Absolon decreed it a real city."

Mr. Thomasen points up: "Look at the Round Tower. King Christian IV built it in 1642. It now holds the collection of instruments by the world-famous Danish astronomer Tycho Brahe. About four hundred years ago, Tycho was a wild man. Keeping his own dwarf named Jebb, Tycho liked to amuse his guests on the island of Veen, where he housed his telescopes to gaze at the stars from his Uraniborg castle."

The students are told, with a touch of Danish pride, that Tycho did his share of drinking. It cannot be kept a secret that Tycho was a bit of a brawler. He lost his nose in a duel, and he went on to walk the streets of Copenhagen with a nose made of gold to cover the empty place where his natural nose used to sit. In 1572, at the tender age of twenty-six, Tycho Brahe found the Star of Nova in the eighth sphere of the universe. Tycho is their national hero.

Mr. Thomasen points up again: "Look, here is the statue of

the Archbishop Absolon, the founder of Copenhagen himself, on his horse." Under the horse's tail, Pia hears Mr. Thomasen tell her to go home. "Ladies don't smoke in the streets," he declares while the small point on his bald head grows bright red. She refuses to put out her cigarette unless he puts out his cigar. Mr. Thomasen, get off your high horse, she thinks to herself.

She tells him, "The boys have to put out their cigarettes, too." She knows her rights. She is seventeen, and she knows her rights. She walks home in a huff. She shakes a little in her brown shoes. Why do I always have to push my luck, she thinks, regretting her ways as she goes home to number 25 in Valby.

She sees Mr. Valde dressed in his tie and suit in line. Waiting outside the bathroom door, Valde, as they call him, finally one day catches her blowing smoke from her daily filtered Prince cigarette through the open window down to Helgoland's Street below. Number-three rule of rules in the Borgerdyd's Book of Rules decrees that permission to stay inside during the break must be given by the inspector, but only after written notice from home.

Pia is breaking number-three rule by staying inside without permission. There is no rule in the Book of Rules about smoking. No one thought of smoking in the bathroom one hundred and seventy-five years ago. Valde smells her breath. He takes her by the ear to the Rector's office.

Rector Helman walks down to his office from the fifth-floor apartment under the roof that he shares with his Swedish wife, whom the students never, not even one time in three years, see walking up or down the stairs. Pia wonders if Mrs. Helman sleeps all day or is held captive under the roof by Rector

Helman. Always a great dresser in his gray silk suit and blue tie, Rector Helman could easily be disguising himself as a fashion model, not revealing his true identity as a prison guard.

Rector Helman wears only handmade leather shoes. His brown hair is cut short above his large ears. Pia smells the hint-of-pine cologne. His blue eyes, peering through his thick glasses, look tired from the hassle of having to deal with her. She sees in them that he does not care if she smokes as long as he can live in peace in his large apartment on the fifth floor. Rector Helman has forgotten part of rule number eight: Rector will moreover be grateful to be informed about circumstances at home and surroundings that may influence the schoolwork of the students.

He tells Pia not to smoke in the bathroom again, and he then takes the opportunity to stress that he's also tired of seeing her in his office so often for all her other offenses, like talking back when she shouldn't and always being late. "And by the way," he says, "I'm tired of seeing you in your blue jeans, too. Do wear a skirt once in a while."

She sees in his eyes that he doesn't care if she smokes as long as she stands up straight next to her seat when he enters the room. She sees that he doesn't care as long as she wears a skirt. "Good morning, Mr. Helman," his eyes wish her to say as she curtsies in her skirt.

The teachers stand in a long row in front of the students. She sees her gym teacher at the end of the line. Miss Lasserup is the only female teacher at the school. Miss Lasserup is young, and she winks and smiles at them while they sing the morning hymn.

Three times a week, Miss Lasserup teaches the girls to throw a ball into the two nets that stand one at each end of the inner courtyard. Miss Lasserup makes the girls stretch their dainty fingertips down to their pretty toes and cheers them on when they run in circles to keep warm in the ice-cold gym hall.

The girls, except for Heidi and Ingrid, are not inclined to bend over in the morning. Ingrid doesn't mind bending over and running in circles. She wins the Olympic silver medal in the 200 meters track in Tokyo in 1964.

Both Heidi and Ingrid are fine Nordic types. Five-feet-ten inches, they stand tall like date palms. Ruddy, blond, and clear-eyed, they greet the world with Helge Rode's song on page 139: "My girl is as light as amber and Denmark's golden wheat, and the eyes shine blue as the sea, blue as the sky that rests deep within it. Princess Tove of Denmark."

Miss Lasserup looks like the youngest teacher in line. The German teacher may be younger, though. Mr. Meyer is young enough to be called into the army to do his duty for his country. "Mr. Meyer, it's time for you to do for your country what your country does for you," his country calls him.

The new German teacher arrives. She addresses them as Miss So-and-So and Mr. So-and-So. They snicker and laugh behind the pages of *"Kleider Machen Leute"* by Gottfried Keller. The new teacher's dress hangs down to her ankles while she teaches them German during the third class of the day. She sniffles into her white handkerchief on her hard chair behind the high desk that stands to the left of the room in front of the seats placed neatly in three rows.

The fumes of peppery salami, sharp cheese, pickled herring with slices of raw onions, and canned sardines in tomato sauce drift through the air. Wrapped in waxed paper, the sandwiches have been sitting on the shelves under the desks since morning. A wooden crate filled with cartons of milk stands in front of them, waiting to be dealt out.

At exactly 11:20, they eat the food they bring from home and drink the milk delivered to them by the class monitor, who is fulfilling rule number five in the Book of Rules: During lunch the monitors are in charge of milk delivery. The students have twenty minutes to enjoy the lunch in their seats in the classroom.

Eating her sandwich in the classroom right after the German lesson, Pia sees Anna-Matilda in the seat in front of her. She sees her taking a sip from the curvy glass bottle of Coca-Cola she brings with her to school. Anna-Matilda looks like the perfect pinup girl for Coca-Cola. She never fails to wear a skirt. Still, soon after leaving Borgerdyd School, Anna-Matilda converts into a flaming feminist and joins her fellow Danish radicals called Redstockings.

Next to Anna-Matilda sits Sonja. Prim and proper, she is the picture of the girl next door. She grows up to become the most unrestrained smoker of all. In no time to speak of, her little fingers with her perfectly rounded nails turn yellow and yellower.

Pia sees Bodil in the seat behind her. Bodil bats her lashes above her alluring smile while learning faster than the rest of them to speak in a melodic French accent that makes the pink ears on Molbo's round face prick up. It makes Pia want to gag when Bodil says "*Bonjour, Monsieur Molbo*." Next to Bodil sits Mina, who polishes her nails the color of field poppies and sends the fumes Pia's way.

Across the room, Pia sees Karen, who is madly in love with

Karsten. She sees Karen feeding Karsten pieces of soft cheese and putting green grapes, one at time, into his mouth. Karen, years later, becomes a dentist and the owner of dozens of Icelandic ponies.

Pia sees Karsten full of grapes and soft cheese. She knows Karsten thinks she is silly and frivolous. She thinks he is an arrogant prig. They despise each other. They never say a word to each other.

Pia sees Lars in the back seat in the far corner, eating his liver paté with pickled red beets. She imagines she has a crush on Lars until he cuts a chunk of her long blond hair off while she is asleep at her desk. In the chaos of growing up, Lars acts the beautiful Delilah. Now, she sees him as the true jackass of the philistines while he eats his liver paté in his seat in the back of the room.

She sees Annette in the back of the middle row across from Lars. Annette gets by with her good looks. In years to come, Pia hears Annette demand in a playful and intimate voice: "Lars, light me a cigarette." He puts the cigarette in his mouth and lights it. He inhales and, slowly and casually, he blows the blue smoke out over her lovely face. Then, with ease, he places the lit cigarette in her mouth, as if there's nothing to it.

She sees Torben in the back of the row, not eating his lunch on the desk in front of him. He gazes up toward Mina. Torben wants to be a pilot, but instead he becomes a lawyer spreading justice among the farmers in Jutland. Torben's adoring blue eyes, it turns out, are color-blind. He won't be able to fly. She sees Bert, who many years later enlighten her by stating while he licks the gravy off his fork: "The boys were afraid of you."

She sits in her seat next to the other twenty-two pupils in

their seats while she eats her dark rye bread with slices of boiled potatoes crowned with a huge dab of yellow mayonnaise. Every day, six days a week, she loves her potato sandwich and her carton of cold milk.

It's Saturday morning. She smells old wet socks in the gym hall. She stands in line in front of short Henning, who three years later smashes into a wall on his motorcycle to avoid a little girl crossing the street. He dies in an instant.

They wait straight and quietly in line, knowing rule number two by heart in Borgerdyd's Book of Rules that decrees that the pupils walk in a slow and quiet manner. Running and playing in the hall and in the classroom are not allowed. They stand in a quiet manner.

She sees Mr. Meyer, his long brown bangs falling softly over his forehead. Standing once more tall and thin in the line of the teachers, he stoops a little. Pia sees his brown eyes behind the square, horn-rimmed glasses looking too kind for the army. They look too kind to read *Mein Kampf* in German. Their young old German teacher is back. The army doesn't want him. He can do nothing for his country. "You're a wimp," they tell him.

They stand quietly, waiting for the order of the day. Rector Helman looks at them through his thick glasses before he speaks: "There's no school today. You may go home." After a moment of stunned silence, Rector Helman continues in an uncommonly soft voice, telling them that President Kennedy has been shot in the head. "President Kennedy is dead."

Oh, my God. Oh, my heart. Oh, my love. Oh, my world. Gone. Yes, he left them yesterday. He left them on November 22, 1963. She sees the black wave coming. It splatters his brain under the wheels of the Lincoln Continental convertible. It splatters his brain across the state of Texas into the Atlantic Ocean.

The wave sweeps his brain up on the shores of Denmark into the gym hall on Helgoland's Street. She looks down at her feet. It lies at her feet. She smells the blood. She feels about to throw up. Oh, my God.

She walks to the Central Station. She sees the stains of his blood on her brown shoes. She sees the big clock hanging from the ceiling in front of her. It shows 8:32 on a Saturday morning on November 23. She walks down the stairs. The benches stand empty. The train comes up to the platform. She sits down on the seat in the back of the train. Pia takes the train home to Valby.

CHAPTER 19

The evening falls black and raw as it only can in Copenhagen when the wind blows icy across the sound from Sweden. It's Saturday, the fourth of January. Mina and I are meeting at the Central Station under the same big clock that hung there forty years before. I see her walking toward me dressed in blue jeans and a short parka jacket. The clock shows 6:00 p.m. She has traveled the cold strait severing Sweden and Denmark to meet me.

We walk up Vesterbro Street to a small Italian restaurant behind Støget. I put my arm through hers. A wet snow falling from the somber sky doesn't prevent me from feeling warm with the pleasure of being near her again. I'm happy that we are just the two of us as we once were long ago.

Eating our lasagna at a small table lit by candles, we talk of our marriages. "It hasn't always been a dance on roses. Jeffrey and I have had our ups and downs like everyone else," I tell her, using a favorite Danish expression of mine. We talk of Mina's divorce from Palle, the Swede she had met in Venezuela when, a few years after graduating from high school, she revisited her birthplace in Caracas.

We talk about the twins arriving sometime soon. "I hope Caron will be a more patient mother than I was," I say calmly. I tell her about Suzanna, who is going to college and has a boyfriend who is thirty-three. "He is thirteen years older than Suzanna. But look at the age difference between Prince Charles and Princess Di," I laugh, making an obviously silly comparison, considering the embarrassing end to their doomed marriage and Diana's untimely death.

Mina has a new boyfriend, of course. "It's funny how we old dames can still fall in love," she says, laughing. She tells me that Britta, her older daughter, is getting married in April. Per, her only son, and his new wife are expecting a baby on the Fourth of July.

Although we take delight in the special birth date of the new baby, our smiles seem a bit stilted by now. It's difficult to realize that we are both going to be grandmothers in the same year. Where did the time go? Where did our parents go? Where are our parents who themselves were not long ago grandparents?

Mina tells me that Annie, her youngest, has dyed her blond hair black and pieced her tongue as well. We shake our heads in bewilderment over young people's propensity these days to poke holes in their bodies. "Our scars were less visible when we were young," I think out loud. Mina flips her hand in the air, letting me know she is not too concerned with the past.

I see Mina frozen in amber, shimmering in the light of the candles across from me. I am again as spellbound by her as I was when we last met in Copenhagen on our thirtieth class reunion seven years earlier. I remember telling her then in my small voice, "But, Mina, you are fifty."

Not quite seven years before, I saw her nails flitter in pale pink. Her curls fell short around her head. I saw the deep blue veins on the back of her golden hand. Her small white teeth laughed as her nose turned up at me. I saw the soft golden hairs on her arm. In a casual voice, she asked me something that did not call for an answer: "So what if I hope that I didn't get knocked up last night after the celebration dinner?"

I was speechless. What do I care if Mina has a fling? What do I care if she sleeps with one of our old classmates? I even understand it. I understand that it's the old familiar pictures stacked away in our minds that make us seventeen again. I know that, however old we grow, we will always have young, soft flesh when we look back with tender eyes. But, my God, Mina thinking that she might get pregnant at fifty was just too ridiculous to contemplate. I had nothing more to say about the subject.

I saw that I did not live in the blue of her periwinkle eyes. I saw her eyes roll up toward the sky away from me. They laughed at me: "Don't be so petty. Don't be such a prude. Don't be such a bore. Details. Details."

"So what if I am fifty?" Mina dismissed me with the tone of her voice. The rest of her thoughts hung between us. Men still kissed her. Men still kissed her golden hair. "That's all that matters," I heard her think in the space that divided us.

Sitting again across from her at the table in the Italian restaurant almost seven years later, I'm reminded of the day, thirty-nine years earlier, when we were only seventeen. The morning sun streaked across the table in Mina's kitchen. Pia saw the soft hairs on the back of Mina's arm shine like golden silk in the light. She wanted to touch them. She wanted to kiss them.

Mina flipped her hand in the air. Pia saw the deep blue veins on the back of Mina's golden hand. She saw Mina's small white teeth laugh at her. The golden nose turned up at her while the golden voice flowed toward her, "No, it's a waste of time to worry."

"But, Mina, don't you ever think about death?" Pia asked her across the table. Mina's eyes shined with laughter: "Don't waste your time with death. So what if we die a long time from now? So what? We are young. We are beautiful. We are seventeen."

Oh, how silly of Pia to think of death. Sitting across from Mina in the kitchen light, Pia knew that the boys would always kiss Mina's periwinkle eyes and that Mina would always kiss the boys. Mina would never waste her time with death. Mina would be forever young.

Covered in short baby-doll nightgowns, their young breasts showed through the turquoise silk as they sat across from each other in Mina's kitchen nook next to the window that faced the pink roses in the garden. The veil of the sweet smell shrouded the table. They drank black coffee with cream. They ate soft-boiled eggs sprinkled with coarse sea salt. They ate white toast with thick layers of creamy butter and orange marmalade. They smoked Prince cigarettes, blowing circles in the air. They laughed, not talking of death.

Instead, they talked of the night before when they moved the chairs and the tables to the side of the living room and rolled up the red Oriental carpet behind the couch to make room to dance with the boys. Oh, yes, they called in the boys to come dancing and kiss in the night.

They talked of the cold beer and the red wine and the smoke. They talked of the music and the slow dancing in the dark. They talked of the moonlight in the cool summer night. They talked of kissing, and they talked of the boys.

Pia looked into Mina's eyes. "What about Latin?" she asked her. "What about the French test tomorrow? What about the black stones in the shoeboxes on Mr. Larsen's desk? What about the ice ages?" Mina flipped her golden hand. "Don't waste your time with worry," she answered.

They saw Mina's mother, tall and blond, leaning against the frame of the kitchen door. Taller than Mina and Pia, Mina's mother also stood taller than her husband, who never spoke a word. Having lost his voice, Mr. Jansen had no place in the family. He had disappeared into the wall.

Mina's father always ate with his head bent low over his plate. Pia's eyes grew big when Mina would sing rowdy songs at the dinner table. She couldn't believe that Mina showed no fear that her singing would drive her father crazy. She couldn't understand that Mina didn't care if she made him lose his temper.

Pia was stunned when Mr. Jansen left the table. Instead of slapping Mina across the face, he left the dinner table when Mina made fun of him across the plate of kidney pie with garlic and rice. Pia could not believe her eyes. She would have happily sung rowdy songs at the table in Valby if she thought for a moment she could make her own father go away.

Pia wanted Mina's father to be her father. She wanted her father to live in the wall like Mr. Jansen. If her father would only disappear like Mina's father, she could open the front door and turn on the light switch at home in number 25 without being afraid of waking him up. Not having to face his temper, she would be the queen of her own light switch.

Pia saw Mrs. Jansen standing dressed in a pair of white shorts in the doorway. A blue scarf was tied around her golden hair and a cigarette dangled loose from her red lips. She heard Mrs. Jansen's deep, smoky voice saying in a lilting Swedish accent, "Good morning, girls. Did you have fun last night?" Pia wanted to sway in the soft breeze of Mrs. Jansen's voice.

"Oh, Mommy dearest," she heard Mina pleading in a baby

voice. "Oh, Mommy dearest. Please, help us with our Latin, and help us with our French, too." She heard Mina's slight Spanish lisp coming through her golden lips. Pia wanted to be Mina's lisp.

"You lazy little things. All right then, go and get your books," said Mina's mother, laughing out loud as she watched them skip into Mina's room to fetch their books. Mina had her own room with a bed in luxurious disarray. She had a built-in closet and bookshelves on the wall. Pia wished she had her own room in Valby.

They skipped back with the books and sat down at the table next to Mina's mother. "Mrs. Jansen, please be my mother," Pia prayed to herself. She wanted her mother to speak Spanish. She wanted her mother to wear shorts at home. She wanted her mother to paint her nails bright red like Mrs. Jansen's.

Mina put her face close to her mother's. Pia wanted to put her head close to Mina's mother also. When Mina and her mother spoke in Spanish, Pia didn't understand them. She wanted to speak in a secret tongue also.

Mina told her that about twenty years ago in Venezuela, Mr. Jansen, who is Danish, fell in love with Mrs. Jansen, who is Swedish. They married in Venezuela. Mina, her brother, and her sister were all born in Venezuela, where they lived until about two years ago, when they returned to Denmark.

Mina didn't tell her that something mysterious had happened in Venezuela. But Pia knew there was a deep, dark secret in the family that remained unspoken. She knew that Mina's father received a letter from the Danish army stating something about his not fulfilling his duty to his country. "It's not important enough to talk about," Mina told her, flipping her golden hand in the air. "Don't bother with him," she said, reminding Pia once more that Mr. Jansen lived in the wall.

Mrs. Jansen laughed. She translated *amo, amas, amat...* She translated from the Latin that flanks of soldiers line up behind each and every hill they can find during the Punic Wars. She translated that the cannons fly in all directions, and the elephants stomp every which way.

She translated from the French about Victor Hugo's miserable Jean Valjean getting chased by the relentless Inspector Javert for stealing a measly loaf of bread. She translated from the English about Ernest Hemingway's old man catching a huge fish in his little boat in the sea. She translated from German about Goethe's Faust selling his soul to the devil to remain young for all eternity.

Mrs. Jansen talked to them about the stars in the night sky when they took a walk in the evening. "See, there is the Big Dipper. See, there is the North Star." She talked to them about Sarah Bernhardt, who was the greatest actress ever to live. "A star is a star," Mrs. Jansen told them while the evening air blew sweet and cool around them.

Mrs. Jansen talked to them about the famous paintings by Rubens and Rembrandt. She talked to them of *Odyssey* and *The Iliad*. She talked to them of boys. She talked to them of jazz. She talked to them of flower dresses, silk stockings, high-heeled shoes, purple lipstick, and red nail polish while the evening air blew sweet and cool around them.

The Swedish Mrs. Jansen, friendly with Rector Helman's Swedish wife, spoke to them about the Helmans. Mr. and Mrs. Jansen went for dinner on the fifth floor of Borgerdyd School often. Mrs. Jansen told Mina and her that they had talked at the dinner table about Valde's fervent wish to catch Pia smoking her cigarette in the bathroom.

They all knew at the dinner table that Pia was the biggest smoker of all the students in the school. But it wasn't easy to catch the girls smoking since Valde was not allowed to enter the girls' bathroom. "We regret catching Mina when we meant to catch Pia," Rector Helman told Mina's mother over dinner on the fifth floor of Borgerdyd School.

Mrs. Jansen laughed her deep laugh, making fun of Rector Helman and his Swedish wife. "Oh, they are so proper. Oh, they are so fine," she laughed as her hand flipped in the air like Mina's. Pia wanted to be able to flip her hand in the air in front of Rector Helman's thick glasses. She wanted to be Mrs. Jansen's hand flipping in the air.

The words and the laughter swirl in the blue smoke above the kitchen table. Pia and Mina pour thick olive oil over yellow egg yokes. Whisking away the hour, they see the magic deep in the bowl. They pour dabs of mayonnaise on little shrimp that fall pink over the dark brown pumpernickel bread out onto the white plate. They drink red wine from plain glasses, like water. They talk, and they eat, and they drink at the table.

It's summer. They lie sprawled on the deck in Mina's backyard in their black bikinis. The smell of Nivea Cream floats from the blue jar into the air around them. White cotton balls separate their painted toes. They have large curlers in their golden hair. They talk of boys.

It's winter. Mina polishes her nails the color of field poppies. They sit on the bed with their legs curled up under them. They lie on their stomachs on Mina's unmade bed, swinging their painted toes behind them. They talk of boys. They talk of dancing. They talk of dresses to wear. They talk of the bottles of Carlsberg beer they have buried in the snow to cool for the party.

It's New Year's Eve. On their way to celebrate with the boys, they take the train to Hvidovre Station. They keep bottles of cold beer in their gray canvas schoolbags where the books should be. Mina is dressed under her coat in the sleeveless blue dress that Mrs. Jansen has sewn at the kitchen table. Pia is dressed under her coat in the black sleeveless dress she bought at a small shop on Strøget. They are dressed for the party.

They are on their way to the boys. Flying through the snow in their high heels, they run to Gunnar's house from the station. They are young and pretty, and they can't wait to do slow dancing with the boys.

They dance with their bare arms around the necks of the boys. They ring out the year dancing cheek to cheek with the boys. They drink cold beer and dance some more. The boys kiss Mina again and again. They fry eggs and slabs of bacon. They drink black coffee. They smoke and talk. They laugh. It's early morning on New Year's Day.

They walk in the snow in their nylon stockings. Their dancing feet feel the snow piercing the soles like hot needles. With the high-heeled shoes dangling from their frozen fingers, they walk on their toes in the snow while they talk of the boys all the way to number 25 in Valby. They walk up the brown stairs to the door on the left, and Pia opens the door softly with her key.

They see Egon sitting in his green chair. He waits up for them. Pia sees on his face that he is scared that something has happened to them because they didn't come home earlier. He looks at her. His huge hand is on her cheek. "You slut. You slut," he yells. He turns to Mina. His hand is on her golden cheek. "You slut. You slut," he yells. Putte tries to hold him back. She begs him, "Please, Egon, stop, Egon."

He does not stop. He throws them all out of number 25, down the brown stairs. He throws them out on the street. Putte, Mina, and she are on the street. "Oh, my God," Pia wails. It is six in the morning and with the hand of the father on Mina's golden cheek, the sun will not rise in the east again. The world turns black on New Year's Day in 1964.

She is banished from the blue of Mina's periwinkle eyes forever. She is exiled from the kitchen table. She is on the street looking in through the window. The cool evening air will not blow gentle around her again. The sun is finished rising.

She walks to Borgerdyd School day after day. With the sweet smell of pink roses blown away in the breeze, she loses her way. She loses her bearing in the dark. She waits for her prince to come to take her away.

Six years later, I see Mina again in Sweden. I see her with her baby girl, Britta, in her golden arms. Caron is in mine. I'm visiting her and her husband, Palle, in Malmö after Jeffrey and I moved to Sweden in 1970.

We fry slabs of bacon. We fry eggs. We drink Johnnie Walker. We drink red wine as if it were water. We paint our nails bright red. We laugh. We talk of the boys who still love her. I'm not in her eyes. I knew that I would never live there again after my father's hand touched her golden cheek.

I see her again in 1983 in Chile, visiting her new home after Palle has been transferred to Santiago by his Swedish company.

Britta is now fourteen, and Per is ten. In her golden arms is Annie, who is four. In mine is Suzanna, who is one.

Again, we fry slabs of bacon. We fry eggs. We drink Johnnie Walker. We drink red wine. We paint our nails bright red. We laugh. We talk of the boys who still love her.

A year later, I see her on Gardner Street in Los Angeles. Mina and her family are doing a tour of California. I see her in Copenhagen at our class reunion in 1995. We make a visit together to Mina's mother, who now lives alone in an apartment in the center of Copenhagen.

I look into Mrs. Jansen's eyes. "How are you?" I ask her. I don't ask, "How are you, the mother of my dreams? How are you, the mother of my dreams who vanished in the night with the hand of the father?" I look into her blue eyes turned white with blindness. Her tall body sits bent in the chair. Her golden hair falls grayer than ash.

"I feel like hell," she answers me, still able to laugh her deep, smoky laughter. She waves her hand in the air. She waves the hand that I once wished to be flipping in front of Rector Helman's eyes.

I weep to myself remembering the hour, thirty-nine years earlier, when the morning sun streaked across the table in Mina's kitchen and I asked: "But, Mina, don't you ever think of death? Don't you ever see the black wave coming?"

Finished with our lasagna, we sit back in our chairs and drink a cup of coffee before we say goodbye again. Having sacrificed, for some years now, the holy pleasure of a Prince cigarette for the dubious promise of a good and longer life, I am not, during this late hour, slowly exhaling smoke into blissful circles over the table. Yet, as I look at Mina in the golden light of the candles, I'm still savoring the moment. Across from me, she shimmers like a maiden frozen in amber.

I see the soft hairs on her arm. Again, I want to touch them. Again, I want to kiss them. But even now, when we are soon to be grandmothers, her periwinkle eyes laugh at me: "Don't waste your time with death. So what if we die a long time from now? So what?"

CHAPTER 20

It's Sunday morning. Pia is seventeen. Walking down Vesterbro Street from the Central Station, she is now a head taller than her mother.

They walk arm in arm past the arched entrance to Tivoli Gardens toward City Hall Square. They see the Town Hall Tower with the clock to their right. It shows 6:55 a.m. They have been told that the World Clock on the tower tells time to within half a second every three hundred years. They see the Dragon Fountain to the right of the Town Hall building.

Tails and claws of the dragons slash the air that hangs dark and wet over the square. They have five minutes to walk to work in time down Strøget behind the Palace Hotel across the square next to the Town Hall building. The story goes that the architect of the Town Hall building had called the Palace Hotel, when newly built, a big unsightly elephant, and without blinking an eye the architect of the Palace Hotel had answered: "And see what the elephant dumped next to it." Oh, the Danes are so funny.

Turning the corner behind the Palace Hotel, they chatter about small things while they continue down the back stairs of the hotel to their lockers in the basement room. Her mother takes out the black uniform dress and the white apron. Pia takes out the baby blue cotton uniform dress and the white apron. They lift out their beige cards that sit in their slots in the holder on the wall, and they punch them into the time clock. It's 7:00 a.m.

The mother walks up to the third floor. Pia continues up the stairs to the fifth floor. She approaches the little room at the end of the hallway. She opens the door to the room and sees Mrs. Olsen in her black uniform dress and the white apron drinking black coffee from a beige cup.

Pia takes off her blue jeans and her green turtleneck sweater. She puts on the baby blue uniform and ties the white apron around her waist. She takes a beige cup from the brown cabinet that sits attached to the wall above the table and fills it with black coffee from the fake silver pot that stands on the little wooden table. She picks up the sweet roll covered in chocolate from the basket on the table and takes a bite in silence.

They start at 7:15. Pia walks to the storage space next to the little room where she fills the cart with rolls of toilet paper and thick white towels. She puts the white sheets and the clean drinking glasses on the middle shelf and stacks up the small bars of Palmolive soap in the container on the top shelf.

She makes sure that the toilet and the tub brushes are in their place at the bottom of the cart. She sees the blue cans of Ajax and bottles of bleach and ammonia. The linen sack in front of the cart hangs empty, ready for the dirty towels and the dirty sheets. She checks the cart again. It is all there. It's 7:30. They are ready.

Mrs. Olsen looks at the list the manager leaves for them at the little table. Room number 505 is empty. The guests have left for other shores. They start with number 505. Mrs. Olsen walks into the room and pulls open the curtains. The gray light floods the room. Mrs. Olsen strips the beds of the dirty sheets, puts on the clean sheets, and vacuums the carpets before dusting the furniture.

Pia goes into the bathroom. She sees herself in the mirror behind the white splatters of toothpaste. She sees the thin arm sticking out of the short baby blue sleeves. Standing a little stooped, she sees in the mirror the black circles under her eyes and the long blond hair falling down her shoulders. She looks down and begins pouring Ajax into the dirty porcelain sink.

She wipes the mirror with a bit of ammonia on the white cloth before she cleans the sink with the Ajax. She wipes the faucets, making them shine like gold. She wipes the orange lipstick off the counter. She looks at the gray ring in the tub and starts pouring in hot water. She pours bleach into the water, bends over the tub, and scrubs it with her brush. She lets out the water through the drain in the bottom of the tub. She wipes the white tub and the fixtures with her dry cloth. She makes the faucets shine like gold.

She looks into the toilet. A brown piece of shit floats in the yellow water. She flushes the piece of shit down the toilet. She vomits into the toilet. She flushes the vomit down the toilet. She wipes the shit off the rim. She scrubs off the shit that festers under the rim of the toilet. She scrubs away the shit that she doesn't want to see. She scrubs away the shit that no one wants to see. She scrubs away the shit she hates to smell. She hates the stink of shit.

She sees pubic hairs squirming like little brown worms on the white tiles of the floor. She takes her thick floor cloth and goes down on her knees. She washes the floor with a bit of ammonia. She washes away the worms.

Mrs. Olsen and Pia walk with the cart to number 525. The guests in 525 have not left the hotel for other shores. They are out seeing the sights for the day. They make up room number

525, she and Mrs. Olsen. They make up numbers 521, 510, 516, 512, and 508.

They stop for a cup of coffee in the little room at the end of the hall. They make up numbers 504, 503, and 524. They stop for lunch at 11:30. They wait for the hot food to be delivered to the little room at the end of the hall.

The tray comes up to them in the dumbwaiter. They open the door in the wall. They see the plates under their fake silver covers. They lift the covers that hide the baked chicken smothered in hot cream gravy and two boiled white potatoes. They eat the chicken in silence. They drink the orange soda and the coffee.

They make up numbers 523, 506, 507, 522, 509, 520, 519, 514, 502, 501, and 513. They make up room number 511. They don't make up numbers 515 and 517. The "Do Not Disturb" signs hang on the doorknobs, so they do not disturb numbers 515 and 517. Numbers 515 and 517 will have to wait for the next shift to clean their rooms. It is 2:35. Twenty-two toilets.

Mrs. Olsen sweeps and mops the hallways. Pia takes the dirty sheets and towels to the laundry room. She counts them before she stuffs them into the laundry bags. She writes the count on the tags and ties the tags to the bags. It is 2:50. She walks out of the laundry room, where she leaves the bags of dirty laundry behind her. She is off for the day. She can collect her pay of what amounts to five dollars.

She walks to the little room at the end of the hall. She takes off the baby blue uniform. She puts on the blue jeans and pulls the green turtleneck sweater over her head. She walks down the stairs. She puts the baby blue uniform and the white apron in her locker. She waits a minute. She punches out her beige card on the clock at 3:00 in the afternoon. She places it back in its slot on the wall.

She waits for her mother to come down from the third floor. They walk arm in arm, sliding across loads of white shit dumped from the sky by the pigeons on City Hall Square. They walk down Vesterbro Street. Pia feels her body break and her legs shake beneath her. She feels the faint beat of her tired heart. She feels herself vanish into the street.

They walk past the entrance to Tivoli Gardens. Their eyes look through the gate. They see the flowers and hear the music and laughter. They hear the roller coaster rush down the mountain and the screams of delight. They walk past Tivoli Gardens down Vesterbro Street. They walk to the Central Station.

They take the train home to Hvidovre Station. They walk through the tunnel, through the park, up the stairs, down the block, past number 19, number 21, number 23 to number 25. They walk up the stairs to the door on the left.

Their legs carry them home, but Pia is too tired to think of her homework due tomorrow. She is too tired to think of Hamlet and Ophelia. So, go kill yourselves, you morons. Poison yourselves, is all she cares to think. Eat your own shit. Poison yourselves with your shit. Eat your own shit that flows in the gutter of the streets. Smell the stink of something rotten there.

She doesn't give a shit if Peter Andreas Heiberg was exiled from the green meadows of Denmark and the duchies of Slesvig and Holstein in 1799 because he spoke too freely in the press about the rotten state of Denmark. No chains held him captive here. She doesn't give a shit that he never returned to the still waters with the thousand ships. Why should he bother coming home? Stay in Paris, you lucky bastard. She doesn't give a shit.

Their legs carry them home, but Pia is too tired to think of Kierkegaard and his asinine fear and trembling. So, go kill yourself. Choke on your angst, is all she cares to think. Their legs carry them home, but she is too tired to think about the frozen glaciers that sweep away the mud and the rocks for eons. She doesn't give a shit.

She doesn't give a shit. So, sweep yourselves away in the mud and the rocks for all eternity. Drown yourselves in the mud and the rocks for eons and eons, is all she cares to think. Their legs carry them home where the black wave sweeps her away in the shit.

She is home, where she sleeps till tomorrow and tomorrow and tomorrow, when the train carries her to Borgerdyd School on Helgoland's Street in the morning. She sleeps, and she doesn't give a shit if they die. "I don't give a shit if you all die. Go, drown in your shit," Pia curses them all in her sleep.

CHAPTER 21

It's an early morning during the middle of August. Pia wakes from her sleep. She looks at the clock on the wall that hangs above her brother's pullout bed. She has to be at Borgerdyd School in less than three and a half hours, beginning her third and last year that day.

Thinking he is almost a man, she sees her brother asleep with one leg slung over the white cover. She remembers something she read about helping your brother and having him protect you like a strong city wall. She wonders about that wall when she sees her brother asleep.

It is 4:37 in the morning. She sits up in the bed that is also the couch. She gets out from under the comforter. She shivers. The black stove stands cold in the corner. She puts on her blue jeans. She pulls her green turtleneck sweater over her head. She takes her gray canvas bag to the table, where the yellow curtains are pulled shut behind it. The bird, who is not Perry, sleeps in his cage under a black cover on the windowsill. Next to the birdcage stands the black phone. They have had a phone now for three years with the same number: 30-01-45.

She sits down at the table on the chair that faces the couch. She sees her father's green chair empty. She opens her book. She reads a part from *Through the Storm: A Churchill Reader*. She opens her book. She reads a few pages from *La Comédie Française joue L'Avare* by Molière. She opens the book. She reads in the *Latin Reader* by Nielsen and Krarup: *amo, amas, amat. Amo, amas, amat.* I love. You love. He, she, and it loves. Love you.

It is seven in the morning. She drinks the black coffee that her mother has left for her in the kitchen. She eats her two pieces of thick white toast with butter. She packs her books in the gray canvas bag. She pulls her blue anorak jacket over her long blond hair and sees the pocket in front of the jacket where the purple stone is long gone.

She walks out the door and down the brown steps. She walks through the park to the station. She catches the 7:48 direct train to the Central Station. She runs up Isted Street. She turns right at Helgoland's Street. She crosses the street.

She enters the black double doors on the left of the building. She sees the nose of Svenningsen shine under the yellow light. She rubs the nose quickly. She sees the white marble plaque with the names of those who died for Denmark.

She turns right. She runs up the stairs. She runs down the hallway. She enters the gym hall. She hears 251 voices sing: "In the east the sun rises...." She is late. It's 8:04. She sneaks into line behind Ole. She hears Rector Helman giving them the order of the day. They listen. They stand straight and quiet. They walk out into the hallway. They walk up the stairs. They do not run up the stairs.

She sees from the stairs through the open glass doors on the second floor the large painting by Stefan Viggo Pedersen of the two young men dressed in short togas. In the painting, the two young men look down upon a bearded man seated in a long toga. Another man sits on the ground looking up at the bearded man. Several other men walk toward him in the background. Streaks of light shine down in the blue sky behind them.

She pulls her feet up the stairs. Rector Helman passes her with the speed of the hare. She puts her hands in her jean pockets to hide her nails polished bright green. Oh, please Mr. Helman, please stop. Please, let me rest my head on your shoulder just for a moment, she wishes.

Mr. Helman is on his way up to his apartment on the fifth floor. He is on his way up to his coffee and his sweet roll. He passes her. He stops. He turns around and asks her in his most irritated voice, "Where is your skirt?"

She aims her ax at his forehead: "You go buy me a skirt, you asshole. Take your skirt and shove it where the sun never rises." She curtsies. She answers, "Tomorrow, sir."

"All right. Good. Tomorrow, then," Rector Helman says as he hurries past her up the stairs. She sees his blue eyes behind his thick glasses. They do not care. They do not see her. They do not see her bones breaking. They do not see her thin arms. They do not see the dark circles under her eyes. They do not see her feet dragging up the stairs.

She continues up the stairs to the second floor. She enters the open glass doors. She is face-to-face with the men dressed in togas. She turns to the left. She enters the door of the classroom on the far left. She sees the three large windows facing the street. She sees the chairs placed in a circle. She sees Mr. Bentsen. She sees his rumpled brown hair. She sees that he has a hangover again.

She sees Mr. Bentsen put on the black record of *Aida* on the dark gray felt turntable. He takes the needle and places it gingerly on the outer edge of the record. The needle makes a small, scratchy sound. He sits down on his chair, and his head rolls down to his chest. Mr. Bentsen sleeps. She hears Aida sing under the sheltering sky. Aida and Radames sing in their dark tomb as they are about to die in each other's arms. Pia is swept away under the sheltering sky. She sleeps.

She sleeps through Latin. She sleeps through Biology. She sleeps through English. She sleeps through German. She sleeps through Classical Civilization. She sleeps through History. She sleeps through Geology. She sleeps through Danish. She sleeps through French. She sleeps with her head on her desk.

"Pia, wake up," she hears the voice of Mr. Molbo. "Translate *La Comédie Française joue L'Avare* by Molière for me. Translate on page 11 right now," he yells. She translates. He says, "You can do better than that."

She aims her ax at his forehead: "I don't give a shit about your *Comédie Française*. Take your comedy and shove it up where the sun never rises." She says, "Yes, sir. Tomorrow."

Tomorrow she will do better. She walks out the door onto Helgoland's Street. She turns left. Today, she does not turn right toward the Central Station. On this day, she turns left. She walks to the corner of Helgoland's Street and Vesterbro Street. She turns right on Vesterbro Street. She walks up Vesterbro Street past the entrance to Tivoli Gardens toward City Hall Square.

She hears the music. She crosses Vesterbro Street. She walks across the tracks where the yellow streetcar runs. She walks down a block to the ABC Cafeteria. She walks up the stairs and enters the large rooms with the large windows that face Vesterbro Street.

She walks up to the line of customers waiting at the long glass counter. She stands in line. She buys a cup of coffee with cream and brings it to the table in the back of the room. She sits down and looks into her coffee. She picks up her white napkin and starts to shred it to pieces. She looks down at the brown table and sees the white napkin in small bits in front of her. She looks up. He is there. Her prince has come. He sits there across from her at the table.

She looks into his brown eyes. Take me away with you, my heart. Put me in your pocket. Hold my hand. Take me away with you. Take me, my treasure. Take me, my heart. Carry me. Hold me. Hold me in your eyes. I promise to love you forever. I promise I will love you always. Take me away to your kingdom, she dreams. She says in her shy voice, "Hello, there. Who are you?"

Who are you? Oh, my love, who are you? Thirty-seven years later, who are you? You are my love. You are my treasure. You are my prince. I see in your eyes Pia standing tall. I see in your eyes Pia sparkling pink in her ballgown. I see her diamond tiara glitter in the brown of your eyes. I see in your eyes the princess that I am. I am there in your eyes. My love. *Amo, amas, amat...* my love.

Ten months after meeting Jeffrey in the cafeteria, I take the last exam of my gymnasium years and of my young life in Denmark. I sit in the classroom in Borgerdyd School on my straight-back chair at a long table. On the other side of the table, my teacher and the two state examiners sit on their chairs. Six eyes look at me. I pick a piece of white paper out of the jar in front of me: page 152. I translate page 152.

Nearly a quarter century after that last exam, I see Mr. Saxø walking into the Ny Carlsberg Glyptotek Museum that stands close to the back entrance of Tivoli Gardens. I see him through the silvery light spreading its glow from the winter garden that grows lush under the dome in the center of the museum. Soft rays flood the tropical greenery planted in the space between Mr. Saxø and me.

I see Mr. Saxø walking in through the large front double doors. Reaching toward the blue Danish sky above the glass-domed ceiling like giant Vikings, the palms tower over him in the steamy light that seethes beneath the white stone arm where the child sits carved in time. The statue of *The Water Mother*, with drops of emerald sprinkling down her cheek, rises from the bog up into the fountain of green, mossy waters.

Mr. Saxø enters the museum that stands a short way from Town Hall Square on H. C. Andersen's Boulevard joining Dante's Square. Stretching my neck to the left from the front stone steps, I can almost spot the Palace Hotel where my mother and I worked so long ago on the other side of City Hall Square.

Jeffrey and I are at the Glyptotek Museum for an opening of the showing of our personal photography collection formed during the years when we struggled as gallery owners in Los Angeles. The theme of "Parallels and Contrasts" echoes the lifeline in the fickle hand. Like sepia gems dangling on the plum-colored string, the photographs hang in the large marbled hall to the left of the vestibule. Pictures of ships and moons and naked bodies adorn the high walls beside the eternal faces of Augustus and Livia and the Egyptian mummies who sleep in their painted coffins.

Anubis sits steadfast and strong upon his throne across the hall. Part dog and part man, he safeguards the dead against all evil. Under his watchful eye, our photographic treasures rest safely beside the ghosts of Degas, Monet, Pissaro, Gauguin, Rodin, Cézanne, and Van Gogh.

I can't help thinking to myself, when I see Mr. Saxø again so many years later, how the skein of yarn shapes the ball of our lives. I see in the eyes of Mr. Saxø no fading with time. He faces me frozen in amber like the stone busts lining the walls. I recognize, as if I had seen it an hour ago, the cast upon his brow from across the desk when I sat on the second seat next to Maria on the left row in the classroom in Borgerdyd School.

Mr. Saxø looks at the walls. He looks at me. He looks at Jeffrey. He looks at Caron. He looks at Suzanna. His blue eyes look at me once more. "You pass the grade. You pass the grade, my dear," he says, smiling at me with his big front teeth protruding over his lower lip.

CHAPTER 22

High on the branch on the island of Tåsinge, the black crow watched Elvira and Sixten embrace in the shadow of the green beech tree. In the rustle of the leaves, the crow heard the shot from Sixten's gun blast through Elvira's beautiful blond head. Then, the black-eyed crow saw Sixten turn the gun on himself.

Elvira Madigan was twenty-one years old in 1889 when she died on the island of Tåsinge. Elvira, her real name Hedvig Jensen, was a circus dancer before she ran away with the married nobleman, Sixten Sparre. An officer in the Swedish army, Sixten was thirty-five when he shot himself on the island of Tåsinge after having killed his beloved Elvira.

Seventy-five years after Elvira and Sixten kissed under the beech tree, Jeffrey and I hear the crow sing on the island of Tåsinge. We are on our way to Langeland to visit my family. We kiss close to where Elvira's headstone stands beside Sixten's. We hear the crow sing in the rustle of the leaves: "High on a branch, a crow, *sim sela dim bam ba sela du sela dim*, high on a branch, a crow sat."

I am seventeen, and Jeffrey is twenty-six. We have just recently met, and I am now walking with my true love along the coast where my grandfather and his father and his father built their boats long ago. We stroll along the coast where my grandfather once sailed his ships named *Ane Kirstine* and *Agathe*. The houses are washed in white, and the red flag with the white cross flies high above the pale-green beech trees. The sailboats sail the blue waters that shimmer golden in the sun.

We pass the two headstones standing side by side in the shadow of the tree. We think of Elvira Madigan and Sixten, as only lovers do. We walk slowly to the other side of the island where the ferry waits to sail us to the island of Langeland. We hear the crow's song across the blue waters that shimmer golden in the sun: *Sim sela dim bam ba sela du sela dim.*

A year later, July 11, betting on the lucky numbers seven and eleven, Jeffrey and I hear Cantata Number 189 by Johann Sebastian Bach, *"Meine Seele rühmt und preist..."* We hear the singing voices in the rustle of the palm leaves when we are joined together by Reverend Pike in the Unitarian Church in Santa Monica, where the oranges shimmer like Christmas balls and where the green palm leaves sway in the gentle breeze.

We marry near the Pacific where the clear blue sky falls into the sea. I wear a lovely sleeveless light blue silk dress with pink rose buttons down the front when I hear his heart sing, "I do. Forever and ever I shall delight in you." He wears a blue suit and a white shirt tied at the neck with a red and blue tie when he hears my heart sing, "I do. Forever and ever I shall delight in you."

On this our wedding day, Jeffrey's brown hair falls short and curly around his clean-shaven face. He does not have a mustache yet. My hair falls long and blond and silky down my back. In my high-heeled light blue shoes, I'm nearly taller than he. I see in a photograph the young blond girl kissing him lightly on the lips. I see her right finger touch his cheek. I see the young girl of eighteen holding his hand. I hear her whisper, "My sweet boy, yes, I give my heart to you." I hear him answer, "My lovely, yes, come to me." I see him smile shyly.

Three years after we married in California, we are back again on the island of Tåsinge. We are back to celebrate our marriage with the family. We are here on the island where the windmill turns in the gentle breeze. We have spent all the money we have in the world to make a visit with the family again. We are young. What do we care for money when we can go back to where Elvira and her lover dream in their graves? *Sim sela dim bam ba sela du sela dim*, we sing in the rustle of the leaves.

Our hearts beat strong and young as we drive a rental car through the forest of pale-green beech trees on Tåsinge. We remember, from three years ago, the trees that grow on the tiny island hugged by land on both sides in the Danish sea. We see the houses still washed in white and the red flags with the white cross flying high above the roofs. We drive the car onto the ferry and sail the blue waters to the town of Rudkøbing, on the island of Langeland. We drive off the ferry. We are again on the island of Langeland that runs thirty-one miles long and six miles wide. We drive through the narrow cobblestone streets, bouncing up and down in our seats.

We see the church to the right where Pia was baptized in the long white christening gown twenty-one years ago. Some three hundred and forty years before her christening, Luther's protestations against the Catholics had made the journey all the way from Wittenburg Cathedral up north to Langeland. We see Luther still hovering in front of the church, posting his ninety-five dogmas on the door.

Twenty-one years earlier, the pastor had sprinkled holy water from the river Jordan over her little blond head in that same church we now see to our right. Her blue eyes had looked up at the pastor imagining, at that sacred moment, the head of John the Baptist above the long black robe and the white collar. In the crystal drop of holy water her blue eyes envisioned his head after it sat upon Salome's silver platter. The child had become a Lutheran.

"In the beginning was the word," the pastor had read aloud, sprinkling holy water on her head. Then the family celebrated into the wee hours while she slept sweetly in the basket in Aunt Misse and Uncle Oskar's bedroom in the back of the house. Egon celebrated the most. He was the proud father. Uncle Thor, Uncle Freddie, Uncle Hans, and Uncle Oskar all made a toast to Egon's good fortune.

"Skoal, Egon," the uncles said as they raised their glasses high. They were the proud uncles, and they toasted one another on the arrival of Egon and Putte's beautiful baby girl. They said "skoal" again. They looked one another in the eye and said "skoal." They raised their glasses high and celebrated into the wee hours.

Aunt Misse, Aunt Eleanor, Aunt Helen, Uncle Thor's lady friend, and Putte sank into the deep brown chairs in the living room. They lifted the cognac that shimmered light amber in the big round glasses. They puffed merrily on their small cigars. They played the piano and sang, "In the forest we celebrate...."

They talked and talked. They sighed and laughed. They sighed and laughed in the deep brown chairs in the living room. They talked about the gooseberries that grew along the green fence in the garden. "Are they as sweet as you remember them from last year?" they asked one another. "They are not quite as sweet, are they?" They talked about the red currants on the bushes that grew thick in the garden behind the tennis table. "They don't seem as juicy as the year before," they sighed. "Do they seem as juicy as the year before?"

They talked about Aunt Helen, who had left her fiancé on her engagement day. Aunt Helen had seen Uncle Freddie walking across the room toward her. His hazel eyes had looked into her smiling brown eyes. She had laughed. He was handsome. She had walked around the table and out through the door. Aunt Helen walked away arm in arm with Uncle Freddie, never once looking back at her fiancé, who still stands there behind the table.

They sighed and laughed. They talked about the boys who loved them once and about the kisses on the green bench under the lilac tree. They talked about the tennis games, the sailing in the moonlight, and the swimming in the deep black sea under the stars. They talked about Uncle Hans, who threatened to kill himself if Aunt Eleanor didn't marry him. "I will kill myself," he cried as he threw himself at her feet.

They talked of Uncle Hans, whom Aunt Eleanor married after he threw himself at her feet. They talked of Uncle Hans's brother, who was convinced that his neighbors were poisoning his cows. "I'm sure they fill my cows with venom," Uncle Hans's brother told them before he was put away for a while.

They talked of Putte and her first baby boy, who had died at birth when Putte was young and not yet married to Egon. They talked about Uncle Thor, Putte's older brother, who had wished to raise the baby, and about Uncle Thor who didn't get the baby to raise by himself. They talked of the baby girl who now slept sweetly in the basket. They talked, and they sighed.

The uncles and Egon sat around the big dining room table. The napkins were back in their silver rings. They raised their glasses high, toasting one another on their good luck. Egon raised his glass. "Skoal," he said, raising his glass until his arm turned heavy. He raised his glass until his steel-blue eyes turned green.

Egon raised his glass one more time before he fell under the table. Taking a few more puffs on their big cigars, Uncle Thor and Uncle Freddie beheld through the silvery smoke in the yellow light Egon slumped at their feet. After an unhurried survey of the situation, the uncles decided to carry Egon to Thor's small apartment in the back of the bank. "It's for his own good," they told each other.

They bent down on their knees, pulling Egon out from under the table. They lifted him up between the two of them and held him up by the arms. Guiding him out the front door, they stumbled down the cobblestone street. They carried him to the bank that Uncle Thor managed a few houses down the street, on Gåse Square.

They dragged Egon through the bank into Uncle Thor's small apartment in the back. They put him in Uncle Thor's bed to sleep it off. In no time, Egon turned his head to the wall, and the uncles again staggered back to Aunt Misse's house to finish off the schnapps. They raised their glasses high, and then all the uncles fell under the table.

Entangled under Aunt Misse's table, the uncles heard the sound of muffled sirens coming through the curved windowpanes from the cobblestone street. Uncle Thor opened his blue eyes wide. Sticking his bald head up over the table, he opened his eyes wide behind his glasses.

Uncle Thor pulled himself up and crawled on his knees to the window in front of the living room. He looked down the street over the plants that grew neatly in their pots on the windowsill. The sirens had stopped right in front of the bank. Tilting his head to the left toward the bank, he saw Egon standing in handcuffs on the cobblestone street in front of the bank. Thor saw Egon's eyes greener than the Dragon's.

Egon's hands were cuffed behind his back on the cobblestone street close to the statue of Hans Christian Ørsted. He stood next to Ørsted, who was born on the island of Langeland and proved the theory of electromagnetism when, in one brilliant flash during his lifespan of 1777 to 1851, he spotted the electromagnetic field in a cow pasture.

The last thing Egon could remember, at this moment next to the statue of Ørsted, was raising his glass and saying "skoal." He didn't remember the uncles dragging him into Thor's bed in back of the bank. He didn't remember seeing corpses floating above him in the green air of his dreams. He didn't remember swallowing sharp slivers of glass. He remembered nothing.

Egon didn't remember that he woke up seeing, from Uncle Thor's bed in the back room, the black bars on the window that faced the street. He didn't remember seeing the green Dragon stick his head through the bars that protected the window from intruders. He didn't remember lifting up the gray manual typewriter from the desk.

Although he had no memory of the deed whatsoever, Egon did lift the gray manual typewriter high over his head. It flew through the air above the desks and the chairs and smashed against the front window that faced the statue of Ørsted. The glass shattered in big pieces on the floor. The alarm shrieked.

Egon now stood in handcuffs on the cobblestone street while the baby girl slept sweetly in the basket in Aunt Misse's bedroom. Pia had become a Lutheran only a few hours earlier, and her daddy stood beside Ørsted not remembering a thing.

Egon was off to the station. Uncle Thor went along for the ride, explaining to the police, "My beautiful niece has just been baptized. She is asleep in her basket at my sister's house. We have all been celebrating the occasion." The police understood, of course. But they kept Egon for the night. They kept him to sleep it off.

He slept it off. In the morning, waking up in his lonely cell, Egon looked around with his eyes turned the color of steel again. "Where am I? Who am I?" he asked, speaking only to himself in his cell. The police let him go with a stern warning. "Don't ever break out of a bank again. Never again."

Egon, in the crumpled gray suit, pulled his feet through the wet cobblestone streets. The air felt cold and damp as he walked back to Aunt Misse's house. In the silence of the house, he saw the newspaper spread open on the dining room table that he had fallen under the night before. His steel-blue eyes opened wide. They read: A FIRST! MAN BREAKS OUT OF BANK!

Putte, Egon, and the beautiful baby girl, who came late in their lives, were banished from the island for years. They were in exile. For two or three years, they were not welcome. The family did not talk to them. It was clear to the family that Putte did not do well. They saw that Putte had no luck in life. They saw that Egon was a disgrace.

Now, twenty-one years later, Egon is back in their good graces, and Jeffrey and I are visiting Rudkøbing once more. Driving over the cobblestone streets, we see the church to the right, and I hear the old song in my ear while bouncing up and down in the car: "In Denmark I am born, there I am home, there I have roots, from there my world begins. The Danish tongue, you are my mother's voice...."

We are back to celebrate at Aunt Misse's house. We see my aunt's blue eyes greet us through her thick glasses. Her hair falls in gentle gray waves on top of her head. We see my father and Aunt Misse both in blue-and-white checkered aprons cooking and chopping in the kitchen.

We see Aunt Misse and Egon dipping pieces of eel in white flour with a dash of pepper and salt and frying the pieces in golden butter that splatters in the big black iron pan on the stove. We see them boiling the small new potatoes and chopping the parsley into fine green specks, which they tenderly drizzle over the platters.

We see the rhubarb and strawberry compote cooling in the white bowl on the windowsill above the sink. The thick yellow cream stands in the glass pitcher beside the sink, waiting to be poured over the compote. We see the silverware newly polished and ready to be placed at the table set for the celebration.

Uncle Thor, Uncle Hans, Uncle Freddie, and Uncle Oskar celebrate. Cousin Anders, who is married to Cousin Leila, celebrates. Cousin Leila, who brought a raisin cake hidden under the red-and-white checkered dishtowel in her wicker basket to the beach where Pia spent her young summer days with the family on Langeland, she celebrates.

Putte, Aunt Helen, Aunt Eleanor, Aunt Misse, and Uncle Thor's lady friend, whom he never marries because he lost his heart to the girl who left him for another, they celebrate. Uncle Thor, who doesn't need a wife, celebrates. "Thor is married to his sister," my mother whispers to me. "He has Aunt Misse for his wife."

Cousins Bert and Nettie, Cousin Leif, Cousin Gudrun, Cousins Eleanor and Jette, Cousins Søren and Pelle celebrate.

My brother Poul and his girlfriend Beth celebrate.

We celebrate. We eat eel fried in butter and new potatoes dipped in golden butter and parsley. We raise high our crystal glasses filled to the brim with ice-cold aquavit. We feel the heat rise to our cheeks. We raise our glasses of cold Carlsberg beer topped with white foam flowing over the rim. We eat rhubarb and strawberry compote with thick yellow cream.

We drink black coffee with cream and sugar. We eat pieces of chocolate filled with marzipan. I see the uncles and the aunts and the cousins across the table all eating pieces of dark chocolate. I see the young Pia across the table when the family last celebrated seven years earlier.

Sitting straight on the chair, the young girl wears her confirmation dress with the small gold cross chained around her neck. Her short blond hair is specially lacquered on this day. Her white-gloved hand lies in her lap, where the little white book with gold letters reading "The Bible" rests in the folds of her white skirt. She lifts up her left hand to the left ear that aches in her head.

From across the table, I see the family raise their glasses high in the air and exclaim out loud, "Congratulations, Pia. You are not less than whole now." The young girl hears them singing in happy voices the words composed in her honor when last they celebrated at her confirmation. To the melody of "I am the oats, and I have bells on," they sang: "To the long island in the south she went to have some sun and some fun. But the novels she started to read at once, and there was no time for play."

Today, seven years later, we eat dark chocolate filled with marzipan once again. We feed Uno, Aunt Helen and Uncle Freddie's black poodle, butter cookies under the table. The uncles and the cousins and Jeffrey remain seated around the dining room table. The uncles raise their glasses high. They raise them again and make a toast "to Pia," stressing my given name in defiance of Jeffrey's calling me Pea.

They make a toast to Jeffrey's good luck. Jeffrey raises his empty glass. He feels the heat of the aquavit. He is finished drinking. He can drink no more aquavit. The uncles and the cousins lift their chins high, emptying their glasses in one gulp.

Eleven pairs of eyes look at Jeffrey above the rim of the glasses. How can that be? What kind of man has Pia married? They smoke their cigars, looking at him through the silvery smoke. Is his brown hair a bit too curly? Is his chin a bit too soft? What kind of man has Pia married? Is he half the man a man should be?

The aunts and the cousins and I sink into the deep brown chairs in the living room light. We raise our glasses of cognac shimmering the color of amber in the big round glasses. The aunts smoke their small cigars. They play the piano while they sing: "In the forest we celebrate...."

We talk. We laugh. We sigh. We raise our glasses in the yellow light. The aunts make a toast to my good luck. I remind them, raising my own glass high, that Jeffrey doesn't drink much. Twelve pairs of eyes, including Uno's, look at me through the silvery smoke in the yellow light. Do they remember his brown hair a bit too curly? Do they remember his chin a bit too soft?

We celebrate. We celebrate till Aunt Helen drags her man from under the table. She pulls Uncle Freddie, whom she ran off with on her engagement day to another many years ago, by his collar to their small red automobile in the street. Off they drive in their little two-seater car.

It hops like a red triangle on the three wheels over the wet cobblestone streets. Aunt Helen and Uncle Freddie take the ferry and drive halfway across the island of Tåsinge before they look behind them at the small space where Uno usually snuggled up on his red-and-black plaid blanket. "Where is Uno? Where can he be? Did we forget Uno at Aunt Misse's house?" they ask each other.

Uno is not there. They all forget Uno. They all forget. The uncles and the aunts, the mothers and the fathers, they forget. Cousin Leila, who brings Pia warm raisin cake when the white sand glitters like silver in the summer sun, she forgets. Pia, who eats the cake and drinks the cool apple juice with the sand sticking to her brown wet legs, she forgets.

So does Uno forget. He forgets. Uno is gone under the table in the yellow light of the silvery smoke. We all forget. "Then the sad crow, *sim sela dim bam ba sela du sela dim*, then the sad crow was dead." The sad crow was dead.

CHAPTER 23

"Are you crazy? How dare you risk losing the house we have just bought with a thirty-year mortgage, and me with a kid on the way," I screamed after Jeffrey had nearly lost his job as a reporter at King Television in Seattle.

Generous but somewhat misguided, Jeffrey presumed that viewers would appreciate observing firsthand the Christian spirit of charity on the eve of the birth of little Jesus. Then, on Christmas Eve, listening to his heart, Jeffrey decided to do a small story on the news about the Vietnam War deserters who, now living on the dole in a cold and bleak Canada, still received presents from friends and family in America.

One lonesome redneck, sitting in front of his television set rather than celebrating Christmas with his children, called the station right after the news and threatened Jeffrey's life. "I'll come over and blow his brains out," he said.

"I can't live in this country any longer. Our civil liberties are being eroded. We're losing our freedom of speech," exclaimed Jeffrey highhandedly. "So what," I answered him, aggravated in my pregnant state while also reminding him next that I had just seen Jane Fonda on the screen last night with Mark Lane. Her constant keeper, Mark Lane had not made the slightest attempt to keep her from saying something she would later regret.

"I see people protesting every day on television. I see Jane Fonda on television all the time, and no one stops her from speaking out," I went on, making my point as clearly as I could in my current state. Frankly, I couldn't be bothered with free speech when my back was hurting, and it felt as if I were carrying a melon between my legs pressing to get out.

Like Jeffrey, I was embarrassed by the guerrilla warfare pursued in the jungles of Vietnam by my adopted country. It was horrifying to watch young men getting drafted and killed by the thousands and then returned home in bodybags. But now, when I finally felt happy and settled, I was not ready to return to my old country, where I had been cold and miserable for too many years.

The Kent State disaster took place on Jeffrey's birthday, May 4, 1970. At eleven in the morning, the National Guard entered the campus, opening fire on the students who were exercising their rights to free speech against the Vietnam War. Two students were killed. Two others were mortally wounded by stray bullets. Nine more were injured. The world was left watching the gruesome pictures of a nation murdering its own children while the Vietnam War kept on escalating to unspeakable heights of carnage.

After the slaughter of students just a little younger than myself, I reluctantly went along with Jeffrey's plan to move to Sweden. While I foresaw the troubles looming ahead of us, Richard Nixon and Henry Kissinger and people of their ilk were saying "Love it or leave it." I agreed to leave Seattle even though I had come to love the place. Besides, Jeffrey had been promised another job at the Swedish Film School in Stockholm.

And then, in late fall 1970, after departing my home in the States kicking and screaming, I'm back in the kitchen in number 25 in Valby. We have sold our house on Queen Anne Hill after living in Seattle for close to two years, and Jeffrey and

I have stopped on our journey up to Sweden for a short visit with my parents in Copenhagen.

I see my mother's flat, tired feet shuffling across the pine-wood floor that she has scrubbed for sixteen years. I smell the ammonia. I see her move to the far end of the kitchen where the window faces the street over the counter.

I see the window from which my mother tossed down wrapped pumpernickel sandwiches smeared with bacon lard and sprinkled with sea salt to the child who threw the balls against the yellow wall for hours.

"Mommy, dearest, please send me down a lard sandwich," the child yelled up to the kitchen window. "Please, Mommy. I'm hungry." I remember the child who ate the sandwich on her swing dreaming of Perry Como in Hollywood. "Oh, Perry. My daddy in Hollywood. My dearest dad," she dreamt, swinging away on her swing.

Today a young married woman with a new baby visiting in Valby, I see my mother shuffling to the end of the kitchen where the gray cupboard once stood. She shuffles to where the milk turned to ice in its bottle and the beer bottle cracked from the frost during the winter.

My mother shuffles to where the butter melted in its dish and the flies buzzed over the liver paté in the summer. I see her tired hand around the brown handle opening the door of the refrigerator that now stands where the gray cupboard used to be. She opens the door, taking out the milk, the butter, and pork sausages wrapped in white paper.

My mother turns around and places the food on the red counter that has replaced the old wooden counter with its cuts and scratches. The stainless steel sink now sits where the iron sink used to be. I see the blue dishtowel still hanging next to the sink.

I see the white water heater that my father placed on the wall above the sink when I was fourteen. It is the same heater that warms the water in the kitchen and in the bathroom that stands on the other side of the wall. I see the water heater that saved them the trip to the bathhouse on Saturdays.

I see my mother walking past the white stove with the built-in oven that stands where the gray granite table with the three burners attached to the rubber hoses in the wall once stood. She walks to the other gray cupboard at the far end and opens the door, taking out the blue-and-white porcelain containers that hold the flour and the sugar. I see the green pickles floating in apple vinegar and sugar and spice in the glass jars stacked high on the top shelf.

"Please, set the table," my mother asks me.

"I'll be happy to," I answer her. "What dishes do you want to use? How about the everyday white ones in the gray kitchen cabinet? Or how about the Royal Copenhagen ones behind the first left door in the cabinet in the living room?"

"Let's use the good ones. It's a happy day today," she answers.

I walk into the living room. Egon sits in his green chair watching the bombs dropping over Vietnam on the color television that stands in the far corner where the black-and-white television of my childhood once stood. I see Jeffrey bent over the crib, trying to dry Caron's tears. I walk to the crib and hand Jeffrey the brown wooden basket with the knives and the forks.

"Here, you set the table. You set the table," I demand.

I put the baby, hiccupping, on my hip and walk back into

the kitchen. I carry her to the stainless steel sink. I pick up the blue dishtowel that hangs next to the stainless steel sink and wipe her face.

My mother looks at me. Then she looks at the baby. Caron looks like an elf in the green-and-white striped cotton suit. "Why is Sharon crying?" she asks me. My mother keeps calling the baby Sharon. It's a mystery to me why she keeps confusing the names. We had called the baby Caron because we like the sound of the Welsh name, meaning vigorous and strong, and Caron clearly lived up to it. But oddly enough, familiar with the Charles Manson drama unfolding on the television screen nightly, my mother remembers only the name Sharon.

My mother has seen the words "Death to the Pigs" flashed in blood on the screen after the Manson followers hanged and mutilated the eight-months pregnant Sharon Tate. A year earlier, she has heard the horrid details of the slaughter of the young wife of the film director Roman Polanski. She knows that one hot night back in August of that year, Sharon as well as four other victims had been butchered in a canyon above Beverly Hills.

Standing over her Danish kitchen sink, my mother is now relieved that I don't live close to Beverly Hills any longer and that I'm nowhere near a satanic cult. My mother has no sense of distance in America, and she has never heard the name "Caron" until I told her over the phone from Seattle the name of her new granddaughter.

"Her name is Caron," I correct her again, knowing it is hopeless. I see the look in my mother's hazel eyes. The look flashes in front of me for only a second. I ask Putte if she ever thinks about her dead baby boy. "How did you feel losing him?" I ask her, a little shy about prying into a past that perhaps should stay closed. "How could you survive it? How did you survive the loss of the baby?"

Her tired hazel eyes look at me through her thick glasses. They are blank. "It's so long ago. So long ago. I don't remember," my mother answers me.

I see the look for only a second. She smiles the little smile of hers. I see her new front tooth where the empty space used to be. My mother opens her mouth and asks me the question I can never forget, "You like to pick her nose, don't you? Don't you?"

What? Do I hear her right? Has she lost her mind? Have I lost mine?

"What?" I ask her. "What do you mean?" She makes no sense. Did I hear it or not? I heard the words for only a second. They buzzed by me like the black flies that once swarmed above the liver paté in the gray cupboard.

I see a strange pleasure cross her hazel eyes. "What?" I ask her again as she moves toward the stove. She does not answer me. Turned away from the baby and me, she begins frying the butter in the black iron pan on the front burner of the white enamel stove. The butter splatters in the pan. I ask her again, "What?"

She turns around toward me. I see in her hazel eyes that she doesn't know why I ask her "What?" She forgets what she said as soon as she said it: "You like to pick her nose, don't you? Don't you?" She forgets the "What?" But I never forget her words. Like flies, they buzz in the empty space above the sink forever.

Thirty-one years after my mother forgets her words, Jeffrey and I walk through the tunnel in Valby. We look to the left, seeing yellow brick buildings where the field once stood empty. We walk past numbers 19, 21, 23 to 25. "Where are the children who played hopscotch on the street?" I ask out loud, not expecting an answer. "Where is the blond child who throws the pink and the blue balls against the yellow wall? Where are the carriages with the babies fast asleep under the feather downs?"

We walk up the brown stairs in number 25. We look at the door to the left and read the sign that now hangs on the door. Mr. and Mrs. Carlsen, it says in block letters. I hear through the door the words buzz above the stainless steel sink in the kitchen. We turn around and walk down the stairs. On the street again, I hear not a sound except for the chirping of the sparrow who sits where I remember the elderberry tree grew tall.

We take a bus to number 8B on Queen's Street. We see the new building that stands in the gaping hole where 8B and 8A and the shed with the two iron toilets burned to the ground thirty-three years ago. Sandwiched between the two old buildings that have stood there for more than four hundred years, the new building with only a number 8 on the entrance door has been built to look quaint.

We try to open the door where number 8B once stood. It is locked. We see the keypad that needs a code to open the door. We turn around and walk over toward the canal. The shops on the street are gone. The grocer, the baker, the candy maker, the coal man with his mountain of coal in the basement, they are gone. The drunkards and the children are gone. I wonder how I can ever be believed when I say that they all lived on the street once.

We look down at the green oily water that floats in the canal. It looks farther down than I remember. How could I

have dropped down that far? Why did I not hit the boat tethered there? How did my hands grab hold of the rope that held
the boat? I don't understand it. I can't explain it.

We take the train to Hvidovre Station in Valby. On the
brown seat across from us we hear two Muslim girls speaking
in soft voices. White silk scarves cover their dark hair. I hear
them talking of the boys and the school in my mother's tongue
clearer than I speak it myself after so many years away. On
the train to Valby, I realize I am now a stranger in my own
country.

I think to myself that even when the circumstances of our
lives change, our desires and our hunger endure and outlive
us. I am reminded, looking at the two young girls across from
me, of the young girl I once was, now thinly shrouded in their
conversation. Their words float toward me; they speak of the
boys, and the kisses, and the old familiar refrains as I myself
used to speak and as I heard my mother and my aunts speak
long ago.

The eternal decree of the lyrics written by monks and poets
eight hundred years ago drifts into the space that separates the
young Muslim girls and me: "Let us be slaves to our desires;
this is the way the gods behave...." I think to myself, sitting in
the train that travels four stops toward Valby, that we cannot
hide from ourselves behind scarves.

We take the bus to Borgerdyd School, which stands in new
concrete buildings in Valby not far from where I used to live.
The old gymnasium has moved its quarters from Helgoland's
Street to Sjœlør Boulevard. The stone column with the six-
pointed star, upon which the bust of Svenningsen used to sit,
has been crushed by a truck in the move.

Svenningsen now sits on the shelf on the wall to the right of the entrance. His nose doesn't seem to shine as brightly as it did before his column fell like dust into the cracks on the street. The classrooms are filled with computers that sit on the light-colored wooden desks, waiting for the students to enter. The old teachers are gone. The hallways no longer smell of salami and wet woolen socks.

In no time, crossing the waters it used to take us an hour to sail across, we now drive over the new bridge spanning the ocean between Korsør and Nyborg. On our way to Svendborg, we drive through Odense, where the ghost of Hans Christian Andersen lifts his black top hat to greet us. "Hello, my friends, I'm here to meet you," he says with a boyish grin.

We drive across the bridge between Svendborg and Tåsinge, where Elvira and her lover dream in their graves facing east. I see the windmill again turning in the breeze. We see the Danish flag flying red and white above the beech trees to the left of us. We hear the crow sing in the rustle of the leaves: *Sim sela dim bam ba sela du sela dim.*

We drive across the bridge to Rudkøbing, passing over the cobblestone street to Aunt Misse's house. We see the statue of Ørsted still standing on the square and the church where I was baptized more than half a century earlier.

Driving on, we no longer hear the voices of the past over the cobblestone streets. The police station where my father slept it off for the night is gone, and the theater where Aunt Misse played the piano is long closed. The mayor of the town is gone. Rudkøbing is now a sleepy suburb of Svendborg a mere fifteen miles away across the bridge over the blue waters that we used to sail.

We visit my Cousin Grete in Svendborg, just a short drive away. I hear her say: "Putte had a hard life. Egon was no good. He was no good." I hear Cousin Grete speak of my parents when Jeffrey and I sit on her green couch in her small living room.

Twenty-nine years after my mother died, we drink coffee and eat butter cookies at Cousin Grete's. We drink sherry from crystal glasses and talk of the old days when we were all still there. Cousin Grete talks to me of the year after I went back to California and the year before my mother died in 1972. She tells me that my mother called her week after week from the black telephone that stood on the windowsill in number 25. "Putte cried," she tells me. "She cried because Egon was impossible."

"Egon does this and Egon does that," Putte told her over the phone. "Egon sees other women. He sees this friend and that friend. Egon plays around," Putte cried over the phone.

"But, Grete," I say, a little ashamed of being told this story, "that is not possible. That's impossible. Egon didn't leave his chair. Egon could not breathe. Egon walked with the step of an old man. Egon did not play around. Egon never played. It is not possible."

"Oh, yes," Cousin Grete contradicts me. "Yes, Egon did play around."

I look into Grete's hazel eyes that are nearly blind. Why does she tell me this? What can I do about it now? My parents are both gone. They are gone.

My mother died twenty-nine years ago. She died the year after I went back to Los Angeles, leaving Jeffrey behind in Sweden for six more months. The light of my life left me then.

My little mother, who would cry watching a Charlie Chaplin movie, left me. The wave swept her away. But her words still hang in the space above the stainless steel sink in Valby.

I hear the words buzz in my ear: "You like to pick her nose, don't you? Don't you?" Did my mother say them? Did she lose her mind? Did my father play around? I see my mother's tired feet shuffling across the kitchen floor. Did she lose her mind just a little?

I saw my father in his green chair again, five years after my mother's death. I saw him on my visit with my mother-in-law and Caron. My father sat in his chair and cried. He sat alone in his chair day after day, missing Putte.

He told me then, "I miss Putte." He told me about the travels they made to foreign lands before my mother died. "We would go away," he told me. My parents fixed up the kitchen and the bedroom. The cracked mirror on the door of the closet was replaced. My mother's front tooth was repaired. "I bought her a ring," my father told me. They were happy. They were content.

I'm sure he did not go out with other women. "What in the world are you talking about?" I ask Grete again.

"I'm sure," Grete tells me. "Egon played around."

She is sure, and I'm sure there are two sides to the story. Were the buildings ever there? Were the onions there? Did the gooseberries grow behind the tennis table? Did the child fall into the oily waters of the canal? Is Pia a mere figment of my imagination? Am I her maker?

Did Grete lose her mind or did Putte? Did Putte make it up that Egon played around or did my mother really believe it? Did my mother call Cousin Grete, telling her tales because she was lonely or because she felt sad? Did my father leave his green chair to play around?

Oh, my God. I don't know. I should never have left my mother to die. I should never have gone away to the faraway land. How could I have left her? Why did I ever leave her? I see the green hat sitting lonely on the sand.

CHAPTER 24

I take my last exam at ten on a Tuesday morning. At two that afternoon, I fly away. I kiss my father goodbye. I kiss his gray cheek. He stammers, "You'll be back. No one can live with you but your mother for long." I look into his steel-blue eyes. I see them love me. "Don't leave us," they say.

I kiss my mother goodbye. I look into her tired hazel eyes. I see them love me more than any one thing in this world. "Don't leave us," they say. I fly away. I hear Perry Como singing in my ear: "...then you'll spread your wings and you'll take to the sky." I leave them behind. My mother stands in her green hat. My father sits in his green chair.

I fly away on Icelandic Air. I look at the seat next to me. I see her beside me. I see Gudrid Thorbjarnardottir, who left on a Viking voyage with her husband, Thorfinn Karlsefne, for the New World about one thousand years ago. She sits in the seat beside me. I see her eyes the color of blue glaciers looking straight through me.

I hear her voice in the yellow light of the silvery smoke: "I will hold your hand, my little one. I know the way. I sailed the oceans only 164,230 moons ago. I know the way, my little one. Come. Hold my hand. Follow me. I'll bring you to your new home, which stands to the west of the moon. I will bring you to your castle. Come. Follow me."

I follow her west. My prince stands waiting for me on the eastern shore, holding one pink rose in his left hand close to his heart. He sees me flying through the sky in my two-winged diamond-studded chariot. He takes me off in his drive-away white Cadillac limousine.

From New York City, rising high above the eastern shore, we drive away in the white Cadillac to deliver it to a movie star on the western shore of the blue Pacific. "All we have to do is pay for the gas," Jeffrey says, counting his pennies.

"Maybe we're bringing it to Perry Como," I suggest out loud to Jeffrey. I'm still dreaming of sharing a strawberry ice cream soda with Perry at the counter in Hollywood. I've never stopped dreaming of going to the zoo with my father in Hollywood.

We drive through Pennsylvania. We stop the white Cadillac next to the trucks on the highway. We sleep on the white leather seats. We drive through Ohio. We stop. We eat hamburgers with slices of raw onion and ketchup and iceberg lettuce. We drive through Kentucky. We drive through the corner of Tennessee to Arkansas. We stop. We eat iceberg lettuce with thick blue cheese dressing. We drive through Texas where the sun never sets. We stop. We sleep on the white leather seats of the white limousine. We drive through New Mexico. We stop. We eat Jello that shimmers in the light on the counter in the Christmas colors of red and green. We drive through Arizona. "Look. Look at the Grand Canyon. Look. It is yours," Jeffrey tells me.

"It is all yours," he says. We drive across Southern California. "Look. Look. There is Los Angeles. It is all yours," he says. I look at the blue Pacific that stretches as far as the eye can see. It is all mine. I look at the palm trees that sway in the gentle breeze. They are all mine. I smell the sweet smell of oranges. They are all mine.

"Look," Jeffrey says. "There is the City of Dreams." There are my dreams. They are all mine. "Look," he says. "There is your castle." It's all mine. "There is your home," he says. There is my home. It's all mine. There are my dreams.

Thirty-seven years later, my head spinning with jet lag and panic, I race down Sunset Boulevard in my green sea-frosted Jaguar. It is January 11. Just yesterday I had returned with Suzanna from a ten-day visit to Denmark, and Caron had called this morning from Kaiser Hospital. The twins have come.

The twins have arrived in regal fashion with the cut of Caesar, and they are girls. What happened to the ill-fated boys, I ask myself as I weave in and out between the lanes. What happened to the two little monkeys who were supposed to be born under the sign of Aquarius?

Sydney Omarr has departed this earth. An imposter is writing horoscopes in his place, and it is clear to me that the world has been turned on its head. I know that Sydney is sitting up above me on the mother of all stars laughing his head off right now: the boys are girls. The girls are two little goats. The girls are not little water carriers.

I run up to the hospital room. Caron lies in the bed wrapped in a pinkish bathrobe that has seen better days. The dark circles under her eyes are bigger than ever, and her blond hair hangs matted around her pale face. She is delirious with joy. Blinded by the breadth of the moment, I tell her that I have never seen her look more beautiful.

"They are perfect, Mama. They are perfect," she cries with relief. I look into her tired eyes. I cry with relief and joy also. We cry together. I take her face between my hands, and I kiss her mouth. I smell her. I smell that she is a mother.

The names of Titiana and Benedicta are written on a label bordered in pink on each of the little incubators. I see the twins curled up under the bright lights. Tomato-red and scrawny, with pink caps on their heads, they look like little hairless

Chihuahua dogs. Tubes and wires come out of their noses and their tiny feet. Titiana weighs about four pounds. Benedicta, her head the size of an orange, weighs about three. "All right, so you're a pinhead," I tell her through the plastic lid. "But I will love you if it kills me."

"This is America," the doctor, half my age, reminds me in a haughty voice after I tell him not to let them go home too early and not to separate the two of them. "In Denmark we don't separate twins," I inform him. "Denmark may not be a world power. Denmark may be a mere dot on the map. But the Danes do know a thing or two," my eyes say, blazing through him. "We are an ancient people."

Caron gives me that look. I know what that look means: it means to keep quiet. It means not to fail her again. I see the cloud move over her face as she sees the cloud move over mine. She sees my eyes turn black. I know she is a new young mother and that she feels vulnerable and scared. So, I give in to her this one time, not telling the doctor, in my voice filled with fury, that I'll hold him personally responsible if anything bad happens to the twins.

I don't declare, "I am an American grandmother. I am as American as apple pie. And don't you forget it." I don't scream at him that I hurl axes at foreheads. I don't yell in a roar that I mean to aim my ax right between his little pig eyes if he makes one wrong move. I don't howl, "Your fat head shall split open as sure as the sun rises in the east. Your watery eyeballs shall roll down to both sides of the hospital floor. The sole of my shoe shall be the last thing your horrified pupils see before they are ground and squashed into the brown linoleum. Your puny brain shall splatter down Sunset Boulevard toward the blue Pacific, and the useless leftovers shall rot into a gray slime in the murky waters under the Santa Monica pier. The last of the muck shall be devoured by sharks, who know full well that they are swallowing a nasty and rancid dinner."

The worm of a doctor has no idea of the kind of grandmother he sees standing in front of the twins curled up in their incubators. Benedicta and Titiana. I look at their wrinkled red hands, and I turn them over. I look at the palms the size of copper pennies. I caress the palms. I wish for Titiana and Benedicta each to have Jasmine in one hand and the Star of David in the other.

The Star of David will bring them glory while Jasmine will be their marker. The Star of David will guide them on their journey. It will protect them. It will shine in their blackest hour. Jasmine will shepherd them across the holy ground between their deepest longings and their darkest loathing. She will stand with her hands on her big hips. Her orange hair will glow around her head. Her brown eyes will glare at them and remind them: "You're a fool. You're the biggest fool I ever see, and don't you forget it."

There are my dreams. I see the sailor lifting the little mermaid out of the canal. Her gray coat drips oily water down upon the cobblestone street. I see the mermaid with a piece of golden amber in her mouth that keeps her from speaking. The sailor carries the mermaid to the white Cadillac limousine, placing her gently next to her prince, who sits waiting for her on the front seat. The prince and his mermaid drive off together toward the blue Pacific.

We drive on the lonely highway. Not a soul as far as the eye can see. I look behind me. I see Caron in the back seat. She is eighteen. Her blond hair flows down her back. She wears light blue baggy pants. Her blue-and-brown flower gauze blouse blows in the cool wind that comes in through the half-open window. I see Suzanna next to Caron. She is six. She wears a blue sleeveless cotton dress. I hear Suzanna humming like an angel in the back seat: *Sim sela dim bam ba sela du sela dim.* I sit next to Jeffrey and look out the window. I see the clear blue sky in the glacier lake. I see the pink and the white and the pale-blue lupins towering at the side of the road. I gaze out upon the lilies of the field.... I see Titiana and Benedicta floating high in the sky. I see Jasmine, tall like a date palm among the lilies, flying twin kites on the plum-colored yarn from her hand. I hear Tracy Chapman's voice singing on the tape player. Her deep voice fills the car with "Fast Car" on the lonely highway. "Fast Car" plays over and over again.

I am the maker of my dreams. I am the marker. I am that I am. I sing the song of the black-eyed crow. I sing it to my mother and my father: *Sim sela dim bam ba sela du sela dim.*

ACKNOWLEDGMENTS

I am grateful to the following for their support and contributions: Susan Derwin and Ronda Gómez-Quiñones; Suzanne Mantell and Angela Rinaldi, my editors; Stephen White, my prince and husband.

—and to Clifford Ackley, Betty Adair, Dyanne Asimow, Norma Barzman, Shannon Skov Davis, Vivian Gornick, Nancy Hardin, Andrea Liss, Tobey Moss, Martha Ronk, Louise Roug, Jon Thurber, Lauren White.